No...

ENOUGH

What Reviewers Say About BOLD STROKES Authors

KIM BALDWIN

"*Force of Nature* is filled with nonstop, fast paced action. Tornadoes, raging fire blazes, heroic and daring rescues…Baldwin does a fine job of describing the fast-paced scenes and inspiring the reader to keep on turning the pages." – L-word.com Literature

ROSE BEECHAM

"…her characters seem fully capable of walking away from the particulars of whodunit and engaging the reader in other aspects of their lives." – *Lambda Book Report*

GEORGIA BEERS

"Beers weaves a tale of yearning, love, lust, and conflict resolution. She has constructed a believable plot, with strong characters in a charming setting." – *JustAboutWrite*

RONICA BLACK

"*Wild Abandon* tells how these two women come to realize that 'life was too precious to be ruled by…fears, by…demons.' While these two women struggle with their issues, there is some very, very hot sex. If you enjoy complex characters and passionate sex scenes, you'll love *Wild Abandon*." – *MegaScene*

GUN BROOKE

"*Course of Action* is a romance…populated with a host of captivating and amiable characters. The glimpses into the lifestyles of the rich and beautiful people are rather like guilty pleasures…a most satisfying and entertaining reading experience." – *Midwest Book Review*

CATE CULPEPPER

"…an exceptional storyteller who has taken on a very difficult subject …and turned it into a spellbinding novel. As an author, she understands well that fiction can teach us our own history." – *JustAboutWrite*

JANE FLETCHER

"*The Exile and the Sorcerer* is a mesmerizing read, a tour-de-force packed with adventure, ordeals, complex twists and turns, and the internal introspection of appealing characters." – *Midwest Book Review*

JD GLASS

"*Punk Like Me*…is different. It is engaging. It is life-affirming. Frankly, it is genius. This is a rare book in that it has a soul; one that is laid bare for all to see." – *JustAboutWrite*

GRACE LENNOX

"*Chance* is refreshing…Every nuance is powerful and succinct. *Chance* is not a novel about the music industry; it is about a woman discovering herself as she muddles through all the trappings of fame." – *Midwest Book Review*

LEE LYNCH

"Lynch, with a dozen novels to her credit dating back to the early days of Naiad Press, has earned her stripes as a writerly elder. She was contributing stories to the lesbian magazine *The Ladder* four decades ago. But this latest is sublimely in tune with the times." – *Q-Syndicate*

JLEE MEYER

"*Forever Found*…neatly combines hot sex scenes, humor, engaging characters, and an exciting story." – *MegaScene*

RADCLYFFE

"…well-plotted…lovely romance…I couldn't turn the pages fast enough!" – Ann Bannon, author of *The Beebo Brinker Chronicles*

SUSAN SMITH

"This disparate duo's lush rush of a romance - which incorporates reincarnation, a grounded transman and his peppy daughter, and the dark moods of a troubled witch - pays wonderful homage to Leslie Feinberg's classic gender-bending novel, *Stone Butch Blues*." – *Q-Syndicate*

ALI VALI

"Rich in character portrayal, *The Devil Inside* by Ali Vali is an unusual, unpredictable, and thought-provoking love story that will have the reader questioning the definition of right and wrong long after she finishes the book." – *JustAboutWrite*

Visit us at www.boldstrokesbooks.com

Not Single ENOUGH

by
Grace Lennox

2007

ISBN10: 1-933110-85-6
ISBN13: 978-1-933110-85-1

This Trade Paperback Is Published By
Bold Strokes Books, Inc.
New York, USA

First Edition, August 2007

Credits
Editor: Shelley Thrasher
Production Design: J. B. Greystone
Cover Graphic: Sheri (graphicartist2020@hotmail.com)

By the Author

CONTEMPORARY ROMANCES as Grace Lennox

Chance

Not Single Enough

ROMANCES as Jennifer Fulton

<u>Moon Island Series</u>

Passion Bay

Saving Grace

The Sacred Shore

A Guarded Heart

True Love

<u>Dark Vista Series</u>

Dark Dreamer

Dark Valentine

<u>Others</u>

Greener Than Grass

More Than Paradise

MYSTERIES as Rose Beecham

<u>Amanda Valentine Series</u>

Introducing Amanda
Valentine

Second Guess

Fair Play

<u>Jude Devine Series</u>

Grave Silence

Sleep of Reason

Acknowledgments

I had all the support an author could hope for, completing this novel with a few logistical problems. My family always steps up at such times, with love, practical help, and hot dinners. My partner Fel, daughter Sophie, and mother Wyn give me more than I have a right to expect, despite the Do Not Disturb signs.

Shelley Thrasher edited with her usual precision and thoughtfulness, making sure I left no sentence open to utter ridicule. Radclyffe is the publisher authors deserve, and I like to hope this equation works the other way, also. When that's arguable, she is the model of grace under pressure, for which I thank her.

I owe special thanks to two members of the NYPD, old friends and helpful readers – Kathy and Mike. I'm sorry the horse scene didn't make the cut. You can guarantee it will show up in another book.

DEDICATION

For my baby.

CHAPTER ONE

W hat's up with the himbo?" Giselle demanded. "I thought we were going to have drinks and dessert, just us."

"I happen to think a beautiful man is the least I owe myself," her mother said smugly.

"How much are you paying him?"

"No one asks a successful *man* if he's picking up the tab for his companion." Nashleigh Whittaker sniffed. "You know something? You think you're a feminist, but you're not. You sound exactly like my mother."

"I'm flattered." Giselle drained her third martini.

Nashleigh wasn't through. "I'm not even going to mention your clothes. They make their own sad statement. Low self-esteem. Inhibitions. Downward mobility. Fear of male attention."

Giselle could not even summon a protest. She'd been waiting all evening for "Fabio" to go play in traffic, and now that he'd finally taken the hint and left them alone, she figured she had about ten minutes to spill her guts. Her mother was paying good money for testosterone on tap; she wasn't going to let the new arm candy out of her sight for long.

"Bobbi and I broke up," Giselle blurted.

"Bobbi…" Nashleigh lingered over the name as if trying to place it.

Giselle gave her a look. "Don't play that game with me."

Nashleigh yawned. "What happened?"

"She was seeing someone else. Anyway, I lost my job." This provoked a puzzled stare, and Giselle converted the whole sordid saga into sound bites any middle-aged anorexic could follow. "It's Bobbi's company. The guy she's seeing works there. She gave him the promotion I was supposed to have. That's how I found out about the affair."

"Ah." Nashleigh absorbed this information with the gravity it deserved. She reapplied her coppery lipstick, fixed her hair, and crammed her nipples back beneath her tiger-print shelf bra. Once she was satisfied that she looked nothing like a fifty-five-year- old mother of one, she said, "My own motto, as you know, is don't get mad, get even. Resigning was the wrong move. You should have stayed there so you could sabotage her business."

"I didn't resign." Giselle wanted to channel the sangfroid her mother always displayed when someone stabbed her in the back, but there was no hiding the forlorn note in her voice. If she could hear it, so could the woman she was trying to fool, and Nashleigh Whittaker had no time for sissies.

"Well." Nashleigh's eyes wandered as she covertly scoured the surroundings. She was pretending to listen, but her concentration was clearly elsewhere.

Giselle straightened up. "I told her she looked old and her pussy smelled bad. And then she sacked me."

"You actually said that?" Nashleigh's exquisite dental work glowed at her from across the table. "You really *are* my daughter. I'm proud of you, pudding."

"These are your commiserations on my breakup?"

"Let's face it," Nashleigh drawled, "the woman was bad news and the job was a dead end."

"It paid the rent." Giselle regretted her comment immediately, so predictable were the consequences.

"Is that why you wanted to see me?" Nashleigh reached for her handbag with an air of relief, like finally she was in her comfort zone and understood what was expected of her. "You need money?"

"No!" Weren't people supposed to scuttle to their loved ones for comfort after a trauma? How many times had Giselle mixed a pitcher of extra-dirty martinis for her mother when the latest marriage got ugly? "I don't want your money. I want…"

Giselle's throat closed. Fabio was back. Trailing after him, a waiter balanced a bottle and glasses on a silver platter piled high with red rose petals. In the center lay a parchment roll tied with a red satin ribbon. The waiter lowered the platter to the table and then poured champagne. He waved at someone and the band switched from jazz to a saxophone-heavy version of "Kiss from a Rose." Fabio hit the deck in front of Nashleigh and produced a black velvet ring box.

Gagging, Giselle plucked at the busy waiter's sleeve and slipped him a twenty. "Another martini, please." Champagne was not going to do it; she needed an anesthetic. She knew she should have left the moment her mother mentioned cash.

Future husband number four had the parchment roll in his hands and was reading bad poetry from it, still on his knees. Giselle wanted to climb onto the table and yell "Help!" Nashleigh was acting like she had no idea the declaration was coming and had not already arranged the prenup. Giselle swigged some champagne before they could get as far as the toasts, then quickly topped up the glass so no one would notice her premature guzzling.

The room swung. Faces blurred like they were flowing across the glassy surface of a lake. The zebra-striped wallpaper swirled into spirals of black and white, punctuated with Art Deco silver and crystal. Giselle was tempted to rest her head on the red tablecloth and wait for the dizziness to pass. Her next martini arrived in the nick of time. She gulped it down as Fabio stuck his tongue in her mother's mouth, sealing their engagement with an exchange of fluids. The ring was on her mother's finger. It looked a lot like the last one. Same diamond, Giselle thought, new setting.

Nashleigh and Fabio clinked their glasses, and people peered around the high wooden booths to beam and join the toast. There was clapping. Giselle resisted the urge to denounce this déjà vu moment for what it was, merely the latest installment in the soap opera that was her mother's life. Born to poverty and ignorance. Raped at fourteen by her stepdaddy. Grandma Caldwell sentenced to life for killing the no-good sonofabitch. The state of Florida had no time for husband-killers, given the man shortage.

After Grandma was incarcerated in Broward Correctional Institution, Nashleigh and her two brothers went to live with an aunt who could not afford college for any of them. To help out, Nashleigh took a job in a gym while she was still in high school. She married the owner, a cheating asshole who made her have two abortions so she would not lose her figure and have to take time off work. The experience taught her a guiding principle she liked to share with Giselle: *only marry a man worth divorcing.*

Giselle supposed the rules were different now that her mother was rich and didn't have to marry ugly older men for their money. Fabio was a handsome, poor paramedic who also did geriatric massage and shiatsu. They'd met on a cruise ship. Giselle knew she had to say something about their big announcement. Her lips felt as numb as they did after major dental work.

"Congratulations, both of you," she croaked.

Nashleigh gave a gracious nod. "I'm sorry if the timing was off. Obviously, we didn't know about your situation." She fondled Fabio's neck beneath the black mane of his hair, informing him, "My daughter's lesbian affair has ended, and she is also unemployed."

Fabio's bedroom eyes swept Giselle with molten emotion. From his chiseled lips came the sympathy she had yearned to hear from her mother. "I'm sorry. It hurts, no?—

when the love is crushed. I see it in you. The heart pines to be whole once more."

Giselle wasn't sure if it was the Italian accent, the European sentiments, or the alcohol flooding her system. Tears spilled down her cheeks. At this, Fabio stood and discarded his jacket.

"A beautiful woman in tears? This cannot be endured."

Ignoring a startled grunt from Nashleigh, he hauled Giselle to her feet. "Come. Your mother says dance is your gift. Show me."

Her mumbled protests fell on deaf ears. Fabio said something to a waiter, who pulled back a couple of empty tables and cleared a small dance area. Fabio sauntered out into the center, tore open a few buttons so his white shirt gapped across his bronzed-god chest, and blew a kiss at Nashleigh. Management switched the session-break music to the Lila Downs version of "Perhaps, Perhaps, Perhaps," and Giselle found herself enticed into a slow rumba.

The dance progressed with the usual teasing body language and sensual hip rolls. Somehow she managed to stay upright. Sliding within Fabio's arms at the appropriate intervals, she made a fool of herself by sharing drunken confidences.

"I don't know what to do. My life is a mess. I have no one."

They shadow rolled, and as Fabio guided her into a Cuban walk, he said, "You are young. These troubles, they will pass. I have three bothers in Verona, all handsome."

"I'm gay."

"Yes. That, too, it will pass. Do not worry." Fabio slip pivoted and they danced in sweetheart wrap. "You are modest. *Vergine*, no? You must choose your first lover carefully. Finesse. Experience. No clumsy boy."

Giselle decided to forgo the technical discussion about what made a woman a virgin. "Are you only with my mother for her money," she digressed. "Tell me honestly."

Affront evicted the requisite brooding lust from Fabio's dance face. "You insult me, but that is not your intention. You Americans. You do not understand the love of a younger man for a mature woman."

"You *love* Mom?"

"It is my honor to do so. Your mother, she is the sun and I am the shadow."

Giselle had heard all she could stomach. She felt seasick.

People applauded as she and Fabio executed a flawless set of shadow turns, then ended their dance in a clinch.

She said, "You're good."

He said, "You have technique, but you do not know passion. When you do, you will dance with your whole body."

"Good to know." Giselle mustered all her dignity for the walk back to their table.

Fabio bent over her mother, parted her burnished mahogany waves, and whispered something in her ear. Giselle could only imagine.

Nashleigh's frosty smile became benevolent. "See what you're missing out on, pudding?"

"Yes," Giselle said. And that was the truth.

An hour later, Giselle stumbled out of the Lenox Lounge, thankful to surrender her senses to the Harlem night. Familiar fragrances soothed her. Coffee. Traffic. Urine. Maple syrup. Fried chicken. She even thought she could smell hot peanuts. But that was a scent of the past, a memory that rose up from the pavements and clung to the buildings. Like so many ghosts of Harlem, it still haunted the neighborhood.

She had declined a ride home. She couldn't watch her mother and Fabio fawn on each other anymore. Besides, she only had a few blocks to walk after crossing Lenox Avenue, and these days W. 125th was an upscale shopping precinct, light years from the scary stroll it had once been. Normally Giselle would have felt self-conscious about her noisy sobs as she wandered along under the pulsing street lamps, but she wasn't the only inebriated pedestrian having a pity party. A man on the corner opposite the Lenox Lounge was yelling about how his old lady stole their kids. He had an audience of homeless people and yuppies. The yuppies paid him to move on.

As he drifted in her direction, Giselle ducked down a side

street to give him time to pass by. Like any other dark, narrow, deserted alleyway, her refuge looked menacing. It didn't matter that Bill Clinton's office was just down the road and Harlem was trendy now. She opened her purse and found the mini-Taser her mother had given her a few months back. Tucked next to it was tonight's parting gift, a check for ten thousand dollars. Giselle wasn't going to bank it. She kept Nashleigh's checks in a shoe box under the bed. Nashleigh knew she wasn't cashing them, but she never said anything. She'd done her bit. No one could ever accuse her of neglecting her only child.

Giselle wondered why people needed the approval of their parents so much, even as adults. And even when the parent in question was just another flawed human being who sometimes behaved badly. Giselle could not remember a time in the twenty-eight years of her life when Nashleigh had taken a break from man-worship just to be a mom. What had she expected tonight— a complete personality change? Nashleigh, suddenly awash with maternal feeling, clutches her daughter to her augmented bosom? Life was not a Hallmark TV movie. Her mother's self-absorption was nothing new. They both knew Giselle came second and always would. Hence the shoe box. Nashleigh thought writing a check proved she had a conscience.

Giselle stopped pacing and stared down at the filthy pavement, angry with herself and trying to comprehend the depth of her disappointment. A handsome, moderately intelligent foreigner was in love with her mother. What depths did she reveal that were invisible to Giselle? What tenderness did Nashleigh reserve for him that she withheld from her own flesh and blood?

Glass smashed somewhere and Giselle looked around. The drunk who'd lost his kids lurched into view, clutching his stomach. He hovered briefly at the entrance to the alley, then staggered to the nearest building and leaned against the wall, vomiting noisily. Giselle sidled backward into a shadowed doorway near a dumpster. As she waited for the man to stumble away, she peered over her shoulder, guarding her own back. All she needed now was to get mugged, a fitting end to a perfect day.

Behind her, the alleyway was empty. No footsteps. The only sound apart from traffic noise was a faint, irregular mewling. It could have been a cat stuck behind a door. It seemed close. Giselle tried the door she was propped against. The handle didn't budge and the distress seemed to be coming from a different place. She left her spot and took a couple of paces back toward the main road, but the thin cries made her uneasy. She turned around and stared at the dumpster. People did ugly things. Kittens in trash bags. Animals hurt and discarded to avoid a vet bill. She couldn't walk away.

The dumpster was too high for her to see into. A few empty crates stood nearby. She dragged one over and climbed onto it. The sound was coming from a mound of putrid restaurant garbage. She fished around in her purse and found the pepper spray that doubled as a flashlight. Pushing aside cabbage leaves and broken-down cardboard boxes, she trained the beam on the source of the distress.

A tiny balled hand waved at her. A ghostly miniature face floated in a sea of shredded lettuce. Giselle felt a hot choking tide rise from her gut. She clung to the dumpster and threw up. Then she climbed over the side. Weeping with horror, shaking uncontrollably, she delved in and lifted the newborn from the shame of its mistreatment. The placenta was still attached. She wrapped both of them in her coat and stood there, up to her thighs in filth, trying to assemble a plan. The hospital. The police.

Suddenly, incredibly, a lightning bolt of clarity laid waste to her confusion and she was as calm as she had ever been in her life. A miracle had happened. A higher power had reached out to her. She was chosen. Filled with fierce wonder, she held the baby to her and stared up at the heavens.

"Thank you," she said.

CHAPTER TWO

Giselle banged on the door of the downstairs apartment and flattened one ear against the scratched timber. She could hear movement from within. "Dr. Redman?"

Eventually her neighbor responded, unbolting his door and peering through a narrow crack before removing the security chain. He looked half asleep. His sad blue eyes were more bloodshot than usual, and his jaw bristled with silver stubble that was probably two days old. He wore a paisley silk dressing gown over drab pajamas.

"Good Lord," he declared in his polished Bostonian accent. "Is that lettuce in your hair?"

"Yes, and mayonnaise." Giselle hugged the shrouded baby to her. "Can I come in?"

"Please do." Dr. Redman stepped back to allow her past. He smelled of single malt, his preference when he was in the money. He stared at the lump concealed in her coat. "Another ferret?"

He was accustomed to seeing her show up with rescued animals. Giselle wondered what he would think of her latest find. She opened the bundle just enough to reveal a scrunched face. "Not this time."

Dr. Redman's expression changed instantly. His brow flattened in shock, and he lifted accusing eyes from the baby to Giselle. "Why in the name of Christ didn't you come to me?"

"I did. I mean, I'm here, aren't I? I came right away."

He gave her a long, disappointed look and instructed, "Follow me."

The room they entered reeked of Lysol and had a sign on the door that read

Dr. Neville Redman
Cash Payment Expected Upon Service
~ No Questions Asked ~

Once upon a time, before his life spun out of control, Dr. Redman had a Third Avenue medical practice and a wealthy Upper East Side clientele. But when his wife started seeing another cosmetic surgeon and his daughter was kidnapped in Nigeria, things took a turn in the wrong direction. He paid the ransom the kidnappers demanded but they did not release his daughter. So he sold his beautiful apartment and spent everything he had left from the divorce settlement trying to find her. When he returned a year later, empty-handed, he started drinking heavily and his license was revoked. Giselle didn't know exactly why. He left that information out of the life story he'd shared with her during their weekly meals.

These days, he worked for a cut-rate liposuction center in exchange for cash and medical supplies. In his home, he provided discreet care to patients who didn't want to take their injuries to a hospital; his spare room was crammed with the contents of one of the medical suites he'd emptied when he closed his practice. A display case in his guest bathroom contained all the bullets he'd removed, and a "menu" of his services sat on the coffee table in his waiting area. This leather-bound folder included pictures of knife wounds he'd stitched up, noses he'd refurbished after beatings, and personal testimonials from locals who bought cheap facelifts for their wives and criminals whose features had been surgically altered.

Dr. Redman took the bundle from Giselle and pointed

toward an examination bed on the wall near the window. "Pull the curtain and lie down. I'll take care of your baby first, then I'll examine you."

She didn't move. "You don't understand—"

"I understand perfectly well, my dear. Yours is a story as old as time. I'm not even going to ask the name of the party responsible." He placed the bundle on a table and carefully drew the coat aside so he could lift the baby from its soiled wrap. "Of all people, I did not expect this of you, Giselle."

He placed the baby on a stainless-steel surgical table swathed in a clean white sheet, and they both gazed down at the pink and purple creature with its spindly, flailing arms and legs. A waxy paste smeared the fragile skin. Birth matter glued black feathers of hair across the worried scalp. A pair of grayish blue eyes were fixed on Giselle's face, at least it seemed that way. Babies could only see shapes, Giselle recalled, but she felt sure this one already knew her. Tears blurred her vision.

Dr. Redman said, "A girl."

"Will she live?" Giselle hardly dared ask.

Only hours ago, this new person was still balled up inside the belly of the woman who had discarded her like trash. Now, here she was in the care of strangers, utterly helpless and dependent. Thanks to Giselle, she would not be found dead by sanitation workers the next day. She would not leave this earth knowing nothing but the sound of her own weak sobs and the betrayal of the one person who was supposed to love her unconditionally.

Dr. Redman drew slightly closer, sampling the air. "Have you been drinking?"

"I was at the Lenox Lounge with my mom."

Tersely, he reiterated, "Go lie down. I'll tend to her."

This time Giselle did as she was told. Sobering up fast, she scuttled across the linoleum floor and perched on the edge of the bed. There would be plenty of time later to explain what she was doing on Dr. Redman's doorstep at one in the morning with a newborn baby. She followed the movements of her neighbor's narrow hands as he clamped and severed the umbilical cord, then examined the baby.

"I'm going to leave the vernix caseosa on her skin for its antibacterial properties," he said, sponging away rotting lettuce and other debris. "You can wash her properly tomorrow."

Tomorrow. Giselle hadn't thought beyond the next few hours. She had planned to take the baby to the police station after Dr. Redman checked her. But now that she thought about it, she could not see the point. Hadn't the poor little thing been through enough for one evening?

Impulsively, she said, "When does she need to be fed?"

Dr. Redman wrapped the baby in a folded sheet and a fluffy blanket. "The sooner the better." His eyes dropped to the vicinity of Giselle's chest. "Any sign of milk yet?"

"Dr. Redman, she's not my baby," Giselle explained in a rush. "I found her."

He was silent, rocking the baby slightly. Doubt filled his eyes and thinned his lips. "You don't need to pretend with me, my dear. Do you think I would judge you? *Me?* A disgraced surgeon who makes a living sucking fat cells from New Jersey housewives?"

"Do I look like I just gave birth?" Giselle demanded. "Have you ever seen me with a big, pregnant tummy?"

The doctor cast assessing eyes over her, pausing at her breasts and stomach. He frowned. "Not that I can recall."

"I'm telling you the truth," Giselle said. "I found her in a dumpster on my way home. I can show you if you don't believe me."

"I believe you. Unfortunately." He stroked a finger along the baby's cheek, sparking a delicate suckling motion.

"She's hungry." Giselle whispered, dismayed. How would they feed her?

"Come into the other room." Dr. Redman walked ahead of her, bearing the baby with surprising ease.

He was a parent, Giselle reminded herself; he knew something about babies. She glanced up at the large familiar painting of his daughter that hung above the fireplace. Miranda Redman was beautiful. Fair hair, an honest gaze, and a big, generous smile. Giselle knew every plane and curve of her face, every pale corn strand blowing from her ponytail. On either side of her stood an African child, holding her hand. Miranda was an aid worker. She had followed in her father's footsteps and become a doctor. But instead of choosing a well-paid job, she had volunteered for Doctors Without Borders.

Giselle had read some of her letters during the meals she and Dr. Redman shared every few weeks, a habit they had slipped into after Giselle made a casserole for him soon after he moved into the building. Normally she cooked, or they bought Chinese takeout, but occasionally he took her to a high-class restaurant, an indulgence he used to enjoy with his daughter. Giselle appreciated his kindness. Her own father had moved to Thailand after Nashleigh divorced him, where he ran a trading company. Once a year, on her birthday, Giselle received a card from him with a hundred dollars in it.

"Sit down." Dr. Redman pointed toward an armchair, and as soon as she was settled he placed the baby in her arms. "I'm going to make you some coffee, then go out and purchase milk for the baby. After she's fed, we'll take her to the hospital."

"You're going out like that?" Giselle asked. "Dressed in your pajamas?"

"This is New York City." He opened an ornamental box on the mantel and plucked out a clump of cash. "Do you think anyone gives a damn?"

❖

Dr. Redman had only been gone for the time it took to finish a cup of coffee, when the doorbell rang. Giselle did not respond at first, fearing that the baby's mother had seen her at the dumpster and tailed her to the apartment. Maybe she'd changed her mind. Maybe she'd abandoned her child in a split second of irrational desperation and had since realized her mistake.

The bell sounded again, this time accompanied by urgent knocking. Giselle called, "Coming," and arranged a nest of cushions in the deep chair so she could leave the baby safely cocooned.

She did not have to peer through the peephole for more than a second to know she was looking at Dr. Redman's next cash payment. She swung the door open and a man stumbled into the apartment wearing a blond wig, a backless pink cocktail dress, and platform open-toe pumps that were probably a size eleven. Blood ran down his legs and drenched the front of his poufy skirt.

"I need the doctor," he said in case Giselle was blind as well as speechless.

She gathered her frayed wits and pointed to the spare room. "In there. Hurry."

She'd helped Dr. Redman spread clean new paper on all the examination surfaces a few times, when their dinners were interrupted by patients. Telling herself not to panic, she followed the usual procedure, wiping everything down with powerful disinfectant and rolling out the fresh paper. The patient leaned against the wall just inside the door, bleeding a pool onto the floor. Dr. Redman always tried to send his worst cases to the ER, but if they flatly refused to go he did the best he could. Sometimes people would die before they would fill out a form. He said he didn't need any more blood on his hands.

"What's your first name?" Giselle asked the man in the dress.

"Prizzi."

"Just looking at you, I have to be honest. We should call 911."

"That's not possible."

"You're losing a lot of blood and Dr. Redman isn't here right now. I don't know when he'll be back." Giselle gestured toward the stainless-steel examination bed, and Prizzi staggered over and lay down on it. "Medical records are confidential. No one at the hospital needs to know everything. Please let me call an ambulance."

The patient shook his head emphatically. His blond wig slid askew. He pulled it off and dropped it on the floor. His real hair was dark brown and cut in a conventional style. He looked about thirty-five.

"What happened?" Giselle asked, craning to see the baby. Was she breathing?

"I'm dying," Prizzi moaned. "Get the doc."

"We need to stop that blood. Lift up your dress and let me see the wound."

"You're a nurse, right?"

"Of course," Giselle lied, bracing herself for a display of intestine or something equally hideous.

"Oh, God. I'm destroyed," he moaned and pulled up his skirt.

Giselle dared a quick downward glance. All she could see was blood and some pulpy hamburger-flesh around his groin. Prizzi looked very pale and his hands shook violently. Giselle stated the obvious, but with an air of medical competence borrowed from the actors on *ER*. "You're in shock. We need to stabilize you."

This observation seemed to inspire confidence. He said, "Please. Can I have something for the pain?"

Giselle looked helplessly around the room, wondering what Dr. Redman would want her to do. He didn't carry a cell phone or pager, so she couldn't call and beg him to rush back home. He said a man working outside the law needed to limit his communications.

"I'll give you some morphine as soon as the doctor has had a chance to examine you. Before then it could be dangerous." That sounded plausible.

Prizzi sobbed, "I should have known I was walking into a

trap. Harlem isn't Chelsea."

Giselle took a couple of sponges and a stainless-steel bowl from the drawer she'd seen Dr. Redman open before he cleaned the baby. She filled the bowl with water, dried her hands, and pulled a sealed pack of latcx gloves from the box near the sink. "You were attacked?"

"I can't talk about it," Prizzi wept. "There was a dog involved."

"You're going to need some shots," she said, remembering what she'd read in the papers about animal bites. "Rabies. Tetanus."

Trying to look like she knew what she was doing, she took a surgical gown from a clean pile on a shelf and tied it over her clothes, then squeezed her hands into the tight gloves. She carried the bowl over and set it down next to Prizzi's leg, praying for Dr. Redman to come back before she did something that would kill the patient. Gingerly, she began sluicing water over the injured area. Prizzi moaned and sobbed about the agony and how he would lose everything and his wife was going to divorce him and this was God's punishment.

"How did you find Dr. Redman?" Giselle asked.

"I paid a hooker fifty dollars. She walked me here."

The congealed blood had dispersed, and Giselle began to interpret what she was seeing. A dog had gnawed on Prizzi's left thigh, leaving tooth holes and nasty flesh wounds. The same dog had apparently chewed his testicles as well. All Giselle could see was a cushion of mangled flesh cradling his penis. Blood continued to seep from the area. She wasn't sure how to stop it. Pressure probably wouldn't work, since there was no single wound.

"You really need to go to the hospital," she said firmly. "It doesn't matter if you're not insured. They'll still take care of you."

"That's not the point," he said weakly. "Just do what you can. I'll sign whatever you want me to sign."

Giselle heard a thin wail and stared toward the door. "Excuse me for a moment. We have another patient out there. I need to check on her."

On her way to the living room, she decided to call 911. It was not okay to let someone sustain terrible permanent damage just because he didn't want to fill out official paperwork or report a crime. There was obviously a dangerous dog on the loose, too. Did she want to be responsible for another attack if she did nothing? She carefully lifted the baby and held her close, avoiding the bloodstains on the gown. The baby turned her head and, with small jerky actions, nuzzled Giselle's breast.

"I know." Giselle sighed. "You're hungry."

She went to the window and stared down into the street, searching for a tall figure in a dressing gown. Surely he should be back by now. The nearest drugstore wasn't far away. She would go out and buy baby formula herself if he didn't show up soon. She hoped nothing had happened. What if he'd been mugged? What was she supposed to do with a hungry newborn baby in her arms and a drag queen with his balls chewed off in the next room?

Giselle picked up the phone and awkwardly tried to dial while holding the baby. The phone slid from her wet, bloodied gloves. Great. It went under an armchair. Giselle returned the baby to the cushion nest and got down on her hands and knees. Steady groans came from the suffering man in the surgery. Frantically, she groped in the tiny gap between the chair and the floor. Her fingertips just brushed the receiver. She would have to move the chair. As she scrambled to her feet, Dr. Redman's voice arrested her.

"Giselle?"

"Oh, thank God." She stumbled across the room and grabbed hold of him in a thankful hug. His hands were full, and she backed away, embarrassed. "I'm sorry. I don't know what to do. A man came after you left. He's in the surgery. I had to pretend to be a nurse so he would stay calm."

"I see." Dr. Redman looked her up and down. Gently, he said, "The gowns are meant to tie at the back, not the front."

Giselle felt weak and silly. She peeled off her gloves and dropped them on the chair. "I was trying to call 911, but I dropped the phone under the chair."

"What do we have? A gunshot wound?"

"No. A dog ate his balls."

Dr. Redman considered this fact for a second or two. "Untidy, but the chewing probably stemmed his blood loss. I guess I better take a look." He handed her the two grocery bags he was carrying and said, "Boil the bottle and nipple for three minutes, then fill the bottle with milk from one of the storage bags and stand it in the hot water. Test the milk on your wrist before you feed her. It should feel no warmer than your body."

Giselle set the bags down and examined one of the bags he was talking about. Puzzled, she said, "I thought baby formula only came in powder."

"It's breast milk," he said. "A patient of mine delivered stillborn twins a month ago. She sells her milk."

"She *sells* it?"

"Two dollars fifty an ounce to men." Dr. Redman glanced toward the surgery. "I bought enough to feed the baby for twelve hours. Call me if you can't get her to take the nipple."

She nodded. "The patient's name is Prizzi. He refused to go to the hospital. I promised I would give him morphine." She felt uneasy. Dr. Redman would treat the guy, ask no questions, and send him back out into the world. He wasn't their problem.

"Thank you for taking care of him. Remove the gown before you feed the baby."

"Yes." Giselle stared at the milk again. "Are you saying men get charged extra for it?"

"Consuela sells to the highest bidder. Men who want to drink breast milk will pay more than women who want it for their babies."

"Ugh." Giselle hadn't thought about that angle. She reminded herself that this wasn't Kansas. In New York City, if you had enough money, you could buy anything you wanted.

"Eat something from the fridge," Dr. Redman added as he walked away. "You look like you're about to faint."

After the door closed behind him, Giselle took off the gown and moved the chair so she could extract the phone from beneath it. Her heart was racing and perspiration made her dress cling. Tears rolled down her cheeks, but she didn't know if she was happy or sad. The grandfather clock chimed two a.m. The baby cried. Giselle smiled through her tears. Tonight, finally, someone needed her.

CHAPTER THREE

"Mirror, mirror on the wall, who wants to pick up Marvin Small?"

Like every other detective in the 28th Precinct squad room, Dale Porter got busy pretending she didn't hear the lieutenant's question. Marvin Small was a stinky refrigerator repairman who lived with his momma, three hundred pounds of hirsute, potty-mouthed, cop-hating womanhood. Marvin had witnessed a murder, and he was supposed to be answering questions and looking at photo arrays. But Mrs. Small thought the city should pay if they wanted the help of her offspring. To talk to him, they had to get past her, and no one was chasing a scrotum injury this close to the weekend.

Dale knew it was only a matter of time before she was fingered as the cop with the least to lose if Mrs. Small got personal. She hunkered lower over her desk, the phone clamped to her ear.

"Porter, you and Babineaux go remind Small about his civic duty," the lieutenant barked. "We got the lineup at ten, and if we keep the ADA waiting again it's not gonna be pretty."

Dale stood and offered a lame excuse. "I got Forensics on the phone, sir. They want me and Babineaux down at the morgue."

"Too bad. I want Small's sorry, fat ass in here, now."

"Yes, sir." Dale dropped the phone in its cradle and poked her partner's soft bicep.

Lewis Babineaux stuffed the rest of his breakfast hotdog down his throat and trailed after her, mumbling about how he needed to get the missus her anniversary gift. As they took the stairs down to the parking level, he asked, "What's the deal for fifteen years married?"

"The medal of honor?" Dale suggested.

"It's not sapphire or ruby or shit like that, is it?" he grumbled. "I got bills to pay."

"Caldwell gave his wife a day at the spa," Dale said. "He reckons she was all over him afterwards."

"Yeah?" Babineaux's face lit up then promptly fell. "Marcia's expecting jewelry."

Didn't they all? Dale had stood in front of a jewelry store once or twice when it looked like a relationship might run longer than the usual six months. She had only put money on the counter for Adrienne. The gold bangle with some tiny diamonds scattered along the narrow band had cost two weeks' salary. Adrienne had been dropping hints about a diamond bracelet for most of the year that they were together. But she seemed disappointed with Dale's choice in the end, and not long after their first anniversary she started seeing someone else.

Dale had a thought. "My sister gave me a gold chain for Christmas. One of those fashion necklaces with a diamond squiggle hanging off of it. Want it?"

"What's the catch?" her partner asked.

"Nothing. It's brand-new." At his puzzled squint, she dotted the *i*'s. "Seriously, do you see me wearing a cutesy diamond necklace?"

Babineaux snickered. They got in a squad car, and he fired up the engine and swung out of the parking garage.

"It's still in the box," she said. "Take it or leave it, my friend."

"How much?"

"Like I'd sell something my sister *gave* me." She checked the road each way. "Clear."

"I owe you," Babineaux said.

Dale scanned the sidewalks for petty crime as they headed

along Frederick Douglass Blvd. "We can swing by my place and get the necklace after we pick up Small. Then you'll have time to gift wrap it."

"Wanna come to dinner with me and the missus?" Babineaux offered.

"Let me think about that," Dale replied gravely. "You spend all day with me, and then I tag along for the romantic anniversary dinner. Marcia gives me a black eye. A good time is had by all."

"Women," Babineaux muttered. "Hey, anything happening on the babe front for you?"

"I got my face slapped by that hooker who stabbed her pimp. Does that count?"

Babineaux grinned. Apparently the case brought back happy memories. He was the one who had noticed the hooker wore the same shade of lipstick that encircled the dead pimp's penis, a fact he liked to point out to anyone who would listen. That was the kind of detail a woman was supposed to notice, but Dale hadn't.

"You're changing the subject," he said. "How'd it pan out with the dancing teacher?"

"Let's just say we couldn't keep in step for the er…tango. So to speak."

They jerked to a halt at a set of lights.

"Ballroom dancing," Babineaux mused. "That's a trip. You never told me you could dance."

Dale looked at him sideways. "I can't."

"Now you're getting subtle." The lights changed and Babineaux hit the gas. "Analogies. Symbolism. That shit disturbs my peace of mind."

"I hear you."

"Oh, man. You got dumped again. That's fucking great."

"Thanks." Dale stared out the window.

Babineaux concerned himself with her unattached state way too much. He was Catholic and thought the least anyone could do was get married and have babies, even queers. He routinely pointed out role models Dale could look to. Melissa Etheridge.

Rosie O'Donnell. Mary Cheney.

"You're doing something wrong," he informed her, not for the first time.

"Give it a rest."

"Marcia says you're taciturn. That's how you come across. The silent type. Women can't relate to that. They have to know what you're thinking."

They were on the Triborough Bridge. Dale took in the view from the Hell Gate Bridge and the East River down to the greenery of Astoria Park.

"People are who they are," she said. "You can't hide once you're in a relationship. It saves time if you don't pretend in the first place."

"It took six months for you and me to get to know each other," Babineaux said. "Now look at you, giving me a gold necklace free gratis. That's your way. You got a big heart, only who gets to see it? Not the ladies you go out with. That's because it's all over before it starts."

"And on that note." Dale used hand gestures like she was weighing the two equally unappealing options. "The continuance of this conversation…or Mrs. Small groping my body?"

"You're no spring chicken," Babineaux warned. "The options start closing down when you're in your thirties. I kid you not."

Dale pointed ahead. "That's Small's building coming up."

The place was a tidy Jackson Heights apartment block. Babineaux parked a few doors away. He faced her, still pushing his luck. "You're not bad looking, not that I know what grabs the kind of females you associate with, romantically, I mean. You hold down a job. That's something."

Dale opened her door. A figured hulked along the sidewalk, coming directly toward them, her curly black wig askew. "If I'm not mistaken, that's Mrs. Small."

"Jesus, she's on the offence today." Babineaux got out of the car, but stayed screened behind his door. "You seen that new detective on Vice? She's single. The boys think she bats for your team."

Dale trained her focus on the woman storming closer. "Talking of bats."

They both ducked and drew their weapons. Mrs. Small smacked something against their windshield. "Marvin's done talking to you," she screeched.

As Dale radioed for backup, Babineaux boldly ordered, "Step away from the vehicle, ma'am, and drop your weapon."

Their nemesis halted at the sight of their drawn guns. She lowered the object she was holding. It was a taxidermied house cat on a wooden stand. There were several others in the apartment. Evidently Mrs. Small liked to keep her pets around after they passed on.

"That's a high-quality mounted animal you got there," Babineaux said.

Mrs. Small stared at the cat and the wind went out of her. "I just picked him up from Mr. Finazzo. He was only ten." Shoulders sagging, she stroked the inert head and emitted a tearful shudder.

"I'm sorry for your loss," Dale said.

Mrs. Small's thickly mustached upper lip trembled.

"Go get Marvin," Dale told Babineaux. "I'll handle her."

She pulled some fresh Kleenex from the pack she carried in her pants pocket and moved cautiously forward, offering them. Mrs. Small's usual belligerence seemed to have abandoned her. She took the tissues without a word.

"What's his name?" Dale asked.

When Mrs. Small finished blowing her nose, she said, "Luther." A flicker of fierceness returned and she blinked hard at Dale. "Cost me nothing to feed."

"A cat is certainly an inexpensive companion animal."

"I got him neutered. That's important with the males or they make a nuisance of themselves." With jaundiced eyes, Mrs.

Small watched Babineaux walk up the steps to the door of the apartment building. "Should have done the same thing with Marvin's daddy."

❖

"You have five days maximum to turn her over to the authorities, no questions asked," Dr. Redman said.

Giselle unpacked the extra milk supply and the disposable diapers from the bags he'd brought in. "Thank you for this. You won't believe how much she's guzzled. Are you sure I can't pay for all this?"

So far she'd gone through about twelve ounces of breast milk. That was thirty dollars' worth. No wonder Consuela had decided to turn her misfortune into cash.

"It's only until you take her to the hospital," Dr. Redman said. "An alternative is the fire station."

"I think it's too soon," Giselle said. "I'll take her tomorrow after she's had another day to recover from her ordeal. I thought I'd go out and get her a bassinette and some baby clothes this afternoon."

Dr. Redman poured himself a fresh cup of tea and added a slice of lemon. "She's doing well, but who knows what was in that dumpster. A bacterial infection is a possibility. I think it would be wise to take her to the hospital later today."

Giselle finished putting the milk in the refrigerator. "Would you like me to warm a Danish for you? I've got cheese or strawberry."

Dr. Redman gave her an odd look. "Are you listening to me, Giselle?"

"Yes, I am. But I don't know why we have to rush. You're checking up on her all the time. If she's not well, we'll go to the hospital. Meanwhile," she lifted the sleeping baby into her arms and kissed the top of her head, "she needs to feel loved. Just look how happy she is."

Dr. Redman sighed. "She's making good progress. But you know as well as I do that you can't keep her for much longer without breaking the law. I've bought enough milk to tide you over until tomorrow morning, that's all."

His tone didn't hold much conviction, and Giselle knew he was just saying what any responsible doctor would say, even one whose license had been revoked. "Fine," she agreed blithely. "I'll take her to the hospital tomorrow morning."

Dr. Redman sipped his tea. He'd shaved the stubble off his jaw sometime between operating on Prizzi and going out to the grocery store. Strangely he didn't look as exhausted as he had the previous evening. Clean clothes helped. He wore a freshly starched ivory shirt, elegant tan pants, and a tweedy sports jacket with leather buttons. When Dr. Redman cleaned himself up, he looked like a man who lived in a brownstone.

"Are you on your way to the clinic?" Giselle asked.

"Yes. Lopez ran an advertisement last week. He's thinks we can make a killing before summer. Figuratively speaking."

Giselle giggled. Every now and then when Dr. Redman drank enough single malt, he rambled about his career. How he used to suck the back-fat out of socialites before big events, so they could wear the designer dresses they wanted, and how they brought their chubby ten-year-old daughters to him to "reduce" for the holidays.

Giselle asked, "Is Prizzi still at your place?"

"No, I checked him into the Harlem Flophouse."

"He's got money, then?"

"Enough to pay me and rent a decent room for five nights. I couldn't talk him into going back home."

Giselle supposed that was a good sign. At least he wasn't out on the streets. She wished she could shake the sense that she should have made that 911 call anyway, no matter what Dr. Redman said. "I just don't understand why he wouldn't go to the hospital, especially with those injuries. There's something very odd about that, don't you think?"

"There's something very odd about most of my patients," Dr. Redman said pensively. "But they're more interesting than the Park Avenue crowd, that I will say."

Giselle slid her pinky finger against the baby's palm, and the tiny hand immediately closed over it. "I was thinking I'd call her Vita. Just while I have her, so I don't have to keep saying 'the baby.'"

"Vita…life. Yes, very appropriate." Dr. Redman sounded uneasy. "What are you going to do about work?"

"I lost my job. So I have plenty of spare time."

"Are you okay for money?"

Giselle thought about the shoe box. There had to be at least two hundred thousand dollars' worth of checks in there. Her mother had probably cancelled most of them by now, but the last few would be good. Perhaps she would bank the ten thousand Nashleigh had just given her. Then she wouldn't have to feel stressed. Babies picked up on stress.

"Don't worry about me," she assured Dr. Redman. "I have savings."

He rose. "I'll come by this evening. If you notice any change in her, or if she feels hot, take her to the hospital."

"I will. I promise."

Dr. Redman smoothed his hand over the baby's downy black hair. "She's very lucky."

Giselle smiled. "So am I."

"Why aren't you returning my calls?" Sandy demanded.

"I'm on the phone now," Giselle pointed out.

"Your mother called me wanting me to check up on you. She was worried."

"Nashleigh doesn't *worry*," Giselle scoffed. "She has better things to do than get frown lines on my account."

"You didn't tell me Bobbi sacked you." Sandy sounded

affronted, like any best friend would when she didn't get the gossip first.

"I wanted to get myself together before we talked," Giselle said. "Anyway, I left a message on your machine right after it happened."

"All you said was 'Let's have coffee.' What am I—a mind reader?"

"Yes."

"I knew she was seeing someone. Who is it—that receptionist with the legs up to her eyeballs?"

"Worse. The jerk from sales who wanted my job."

"A man? Bobbi dumped you for a man?"

"Now do you see why I needed a couple of days to myself?"

"Jesus, that toxic whore."

Sandy had always hated Bobbi. The feeling was mutual. Giselle had tried to play their friendship down for the two years she and Bobbi were together, so that Bobbi wouldn't delete Sandy's voice mail and be rude to her when they all went out together.

Giselle said, "She's really not that bad. Ever since she turned forty she's been weird. It's some kind of mid-life crisis, I think."

"That's supposed to happen when you're fifty, and most people don't suddenly decide to trade in their sexuality." Sandy sighed loudly. "The fact is she used you. She got all the contacts she could, thanks to your mom, then moved on."

"Relationships end," Giselle said. "Sometimes people just grow apart."

"You have to stop defending her, Zelly. She's a sleazy, conniving bitch. It's just as simple as that. And you know what else I heard?"

"I guess it's no good saying I'm not interested."

Sandy replied, "Totally pointless. I heard she's having financial problems. That guy you're talking about. That's Bentley Johnson's son. I bet you didn't know that, did you?"

"Who's Bentley Johnson?"

"You are so out of touch. Oh, what does it matter? The point is you're single again, and I'm glad she's out of your life. She only made you feel bad about yourself."

"What are you talking about?"

"Zelly, you've hardly been out of the house in two years except to go to work."

"I've been busy."

"You've been depressed. I had tickets to U2 at Madison Square Garden, remember? And I ended up going with the nerd who fixes our server because you were 'tired.'"

"I'd only been with her for a couple of months then," Giselle pointed out reasonably. "And I was working two jobs. I really *was* tired."

"Listen to yourself. I tried to warn you about her. But what do I know? I'm only your best friend who has known you since we were three. Admit it. She made you feel ugly and stupid."

"Another person can't make you feel those things," Giselle objected.

"Oh, really? You don't think a partner can affect the way you see yourself? What about Emma?"

Giselle rolled her eyes. Emma was a mutual friend who had always been on the mousy side. Then she got with a woman who worked in the TV industry. They were madly in love and the transformation in Emma was incredible. She lost twenty pounds, worked out, wore hot clothes, and got her hair lightened. And none of this seemed to be a consequence of image-pressure from the girlfriend. It was obvious from Day One that Emma had met Ms. Right and that this woman had simply invited her to be all she could be. Every time Giselle thought about it, she felt sick. Irritated, she ran her fingers back and forth along her upper lip, a nervous habit she'd developed as a child. The urge had returned recently and she was trying to be more aware of it, so she could stamp it out before it became unconscious.

"The big difference between me and Emma," she said, "is that Emma was already beautiful and perfect. All she needed was for someone to help her see who she really was so she could blossom."

"The other big difference is that she didn't think she had to settle for the first woman who took an interest in her in case there weren't any more." Sandy groaned. "I'm sorry. Me and my big mouth."

"Is there anything else you wanted to talk about other than my bad taste in women and lack of self-esteem?" Giselle asked.

"Don't be mad at me. You know I worry about you, that's all. I hate seeing you unhappy and I hate that Bobbi hurt you."

"Actually, I'm glad it happened," Giselle said. "I need to toughen up and learn to be less gullible."

"No, you don't. The world needs all the kindhearted people it can get. I should have been more direct with you. I had a feeling about her but I was trying to mind my own business."

"My relationships are not your responsibility," Giselle said, and she meant it. "You're right about one thing, though. Bobbi made me feel bad about myself, and I think she did it deliberately. She wanted to make me dependent and grateful so she could do whatever she liked."

When they had their big fight, Bobbi had started out expecting Giselle to accept the affair. She seemed to think their relationship could continue unchanged. Her exact words were "You're not going to get anyone else. Look in the mirror."

"Want sushi for dinner?" Sandy asked.

"Not tonight. I have things to do."

"This is exactly what I'm talking about," Sandy said. "You have no job. No partner. No commitments. But you can't come and eat sushi—your favorite—with your best friend."

"I wish I could." Giselle straightened Vita's blanket. "But I have a prior commitment. I'll take a rain check and we can go out next week. I'll even endure a club."

"I'm on my way over," Sandy said.

"No." It came out too sharply. "I mean, there's no need. I'm fine."

"I promised your mom I would look in on you."

"I only saw Mom two days ago. This is ridiculous."

"She said you banked one of her checks. You have to admit that's quite a change in behavior."

"So what? I just lost my job."

"It's suspicious," Sandy said. "I'll see you in fifteen minutes. Don't pretend you can't hear me knocking, either."

"No, wait. Listen to me, Sandy. I need some space, that's all. It's no big deal. Please, just call me tomorrow."

"Okay, have your space, but I'm coming by tomorrow. I should have done this two years ago. Call it an intervention."

Giselle knew when Sandy was not going to budge. Challenging her only made her all the more determined to win. She wasn't a DA for nothing. Frustrated, she barked, "Whatever," and dumped the phone in its cradle.

At first she felt a fluttery panic in her belly, then she stared at Vita and a sense of well-being came over her. Suddenly she was clearheaded and in control. Her agitated breathing calmed, and the muscles in her face relaxed into serenity. Why shouldn't she have a baby in her apartment? She could be helping some neighbors out or minding a friend's baby for a few hours so she could apply for a job. People took care of other people's children all the time. Just because Sandy never saw her do so didn't mean she was not acquainted with any.

"I'm taking care of Vita for friends from Brooklyn," she informed the imaginary Sandy sitting opposite her. "I like babysitting."

CHAPTER FOUR

Y ou're the worst liar I know," Sandy said, taking stock of the refrigerator contents. "I count four bottles of milk, and you have three diapers in the trash."

"I change her quite often. She's little. That's what you're supposed to do."

"Who leaves a newborn baby with a friend overnight?"

Giselle adopted a vague air. "Maybe they just need some alone time."

"For what? Hot sex?"

"I think they were planning a special dinner."

"A woman that just gave birth forty-eight hours ago was busting her ass to sit on a hard chair in a restaurant? No, trust me, women in that situation…they want to sit in a rubber donut ring, without their panties."

"I'm sure they'll show up soon." Giselle cast a quick guilty look at the wall clock. It was two in the afternoon. Sandy was incredulous for good reason.

"Let's find out. Being brand-new parents and all, they'll have their cell phone with them. People are terrified to leave their two-day-old baby with someone else, let alone for a whole night." Sandy smiled coolly. "What's their number?"

Giselle said, "Keep your voice down. You'll wake her up."

Sandy tapped her foot. She had her hands on her hips. As usual, she looked effortlessly gorgeous with her short black hair freshly cut and her toffee-eyed gaze enhanced with kohl. A cream shell and tailored pants set off her coloring and shape to full advantage, and, as always, she wore the heavy gold earrings she had inherited from her Creole grandma.

Gisclle used to be amazed that Sandy had ever become her best friend. They were complete opposites. Sandy was extroverted, incredibly smart, beautiful, witty, and successful; Giselle was quiet, plain, and overly sensitive. Lately, however, she'd figured out that she offered something Sandy needed. Out in the world, where people expected so much from her, Sandy had to be "on" all the time. When they were together, she could unwind and be herself. They knew each other too well for pretense.

Which was probably why Sandy demanded, "Okay, where did you get her?"

Giselle gave up the bullshit and admitted, "I found her in a dumpster."

"Oh, my God." Sandy's mouth trembled. Under the tough, glossy exterior, she was easily touched. "How could anyone do that?"

"I was drunk and a mess." Giselle hastened to explain herself. "I couldn't go to the police station in that condition. So I brought her home."

Sandy threw her hands up in the air. "What if she'd died?"

"I took her to Dr. Redman," Giselle replied calmly. "He said she was fine. He even got real breast milk for her from a lady who normally sells it to perverts."

Sandy covered her ears. "Enough."

She preferred not to know anything about Dr. Redman or other illegal activities in the neighborhood unless the crimes were serious. Giselle contemplated telling her what had happened to Prizzi. The attack was obviously a hate crime. She wasn't sure if Prizzi was a transsexual or a cross-dresser, but the distinction was meaningless. A bigot had set his dog onto a stranger who looked different. Giselle wished she had called the police, yet she wasn't really sure what would have happened if she had. Would they try to find the attacker? Did they take crimes against people like Prizzi seriously, or would they secretly find the injuries funny?

"I think I'd better take her to the police for you," Sandy said.

"No. I'll deal with it."

Sandy searched her face. "You have to hand her over, Zelly. You know that, don't you?"

"Who says I have to?" Giselle stared down at Vita. "No one knows anything about her except you and Dr. Redman."

Sandy's expression grew wary. She loafed into the living room and sank into the spare armchair. Sliding the pumps from her feet, she said, "Tell me what's on your mind."

Giselle perched on the chair next to Sandy's. "I want to keep her."

"Why?" There was no accusation in her tone. She sounded baffled.

"I think I found her for a reason. Her mother threw her away, a living, beautiful little baby. I found her in a dumpster. *A dumpster!* Think about it. What kind of mother does that?" She heard her own speech distorting with emotion. Forcing herself to slow down, she said, "I'd be a better mother than that."

Sandy took her hand. "Yes, you would. One day, when the time is right, I can see you with a good woman and some kids."

"I don't think it's going to happen," Giselle said despondently. "I'm not like you. I don't have women breaking my door down, and I don't want to be 'out there' looking. People know when you're desperate."

"There's plenty of time. You're not even thirty. And you need to get your life together before you bring a child into it, partner or not."

Giselle took her hand back. She felt defensive, yet at the same time she knew Sandy was speaking the truth. Her life was not together. She'd graduated from Brooklyn College with a fine-arts degree that proved she could construct a grammatical sentence and discuss watercolor technique. Since then, she'd held down three poorly paid jobs in what could generously be described as "management."

The only thing she really enjoyed doing was portrait painting, a hobby she could not pursue with real commitment because she had neither the time nor the space. She could not afford to rent a studio, or even to share one. And what would be the point? Bobbi knew people in the art business, and she said there was no way they would look at amateur works like hers. Giselle kept her paintings to herself or gave them away as gifts to friends like Dr. Redman, who were nice enough to say they were good.

"How long have you had her?" Sandy asked.

"Since Friday night."

"It's now Sunday afternoon."

"I know."

"You have until Wednesday, because they'll think you're the mother and you won't have to answer any questions. After that you're a kidnapper."

"Why? If I took her to the police, wouldn't they give her to a foster mother until she got adopted? That's all I'm doing."

"A foster mother is inside the system and everyone knows she has the child," Sandy said. "You can't just find a baby and keep it. Anything could have happened. What if she was stolen from her mother, and the thief got worried and dropped her in the dumpster? You don't know the circumstances. That's why we have laws."

Giselle shuddered at the thought that a perfectly good mother could be losing her mind right now, searching for her baby. Sandy was right. She had to give Vita up. A noisy sob rose from her throat and she burbled, "Take her, then."

Sandy hugged her. "I have an idea. Why don't you spend the rest of the day with her, and I'll come back tonight with a detective I know. She'll take the baby and deal with all the formalities."

Giselle wept against Sandy's good-smelling neck for a few minutes, mopping the tears with her shirtsleeve so they wouldn't stain Sandy's pale shell. Eventually, she said, "I'll have her ready to leave around eight."

Sandy patted her the way she used to when Giselle got bullied at school. "Everything will work out fine, I promise."

Giselle seriously doubted it, but she pulled herself together and saw her best friend to the door. When Sandy had gone, she returned to the living room and stared blankly at the wall. In a few hours Vita would be gone and she would never know the woman who had rescued her, whose skin was the first she really smelled.

Giselle wallowed in self-pity for a few seconds before she was seized with an idea. Cursing the opportunity she'd squandered so far, she found the one fresh canvas she'd been saving for a special portrait and hauled her easel and palette out from the large sideboard that occupied the longest wall in her apartment. She didn't have much time, but she could take photographs to record composition, value patterns, and lighting, and then complete a basic wash-in.

Even after Vita was gone, she could keep working on the portrait, converting memory to brushstroke. It was better than nothing.

❖

"Who are you?"

"I'm Dale, Mom. Your daughter."

"What do you want?"

"I came to do your yard." Dale stared out the leaded living-room windows past the willows to the Hudson River. It was time to hire someone to shape the trees. She couldn't do everything herself, and the Tarrytown property needed more than the few hours each week she could spare between shifts.

"Where's Penelope?" her mother asked.

"She's not coming today."

"Why not?"

Good question. Dale contemplated several answers: *She's*

too busy shopping. She's at the day spa. She's having her Botox done. Searching lucklessly for an original excuse, she said, "I guess she has a lot to do, with the wedding coming up."

Ophelia Williams, the Porters' housekeeper, angled her chin. "Mnhmn. Mrs. Avaryss, she got *sooo* much to think about, being the mother of the groom and all. Wedding only six months away. Phew! Must be making her crazy. She got that dress to buy and the wedding gift. Oh, sweet Jesus."

Dale's mom interrupted the sharp-tongued monologue. "I like weddings."

"This one is going to be very expensive," Dale assured her.

She didn't know the full details yet, but Penelope had always mistaken money for class. She and the bride's mother, a kindred spirit, had been desperate to eclipse each other's pretensions ever since their precious kids started dating. Penelope had unearthed the real story of her rival's past by sending a private investigator to Florida to check into her background. Although she trumpeted her discoveries to Dale, she hadn't said a word to anyone else. She was, she'd told Dale, biding her time for the "right moment."

Mrs. van Label had clawed her way up from a trailer park in Opa-Locka, a past she referred to as "my childhood in Coral Gables." At eighteen she'd married a fifty-eight-year-old patron of the bar where she lap danced under a fake ID. He died in a robbery, leaving her with enough life-insurance money to reinvent herself in Los Angeles. She duly became pregnant by Elaine's father, a celebrity divorce lawyer. Their one daughter enjoyed the childhood Mrs. van Label wished she could have had herself. Now she was in possession of the ultimate trump card—a wedding—and Penelope was seething with the malice of a beauty queen who only made runner-up. Things were going to get ugly.

"What wedding?" Laurel Porter belatedly inquired.

"Wayne and Elaine," Dale said. "Wayne is your grandson."

Laurel frowned. "Elaine?"

"Elaine van Label." Dale tried to come up with a description that would do justice to Penelope's future daughter-in-law. Paris Hilton was a shining example of selflessness by contrast with Elaine. She pointed at a large framed photograph on the mantel. "That's their engagement picture, remember. She's the blonde."

A smile of recognition lifted her mom's sagging features. "Oh, yes. Penelope says she dresses like a cheap slut."

"She and Wayne suit each other," Dale observed reasonably. Penelope had instilled in her son the proud values that reflected her own. "He cares as much about money and appearance as she does, if that's humanly possible."

"Wayne is a very successful young man," Laurel declared sagely.

"Assuming Kenneth Lay is the benchmark," Dale said. As far as she could recall, her nephew had nothing but admiration for the much-maligned head honchos of Enron. "But whatever."

"You sound like your father."

"Thank you." Sorrow crushed the breath from Dale's lungs. Her dad had died five years earlier. She never stopped missing him.

"Penelope says you're getting a wedding invitation."

"Whew. I can sleep easy," Dale muttered.

"She doesn't want you to bring a date."

"Just so you know," Dale said blandly, "Penelope is planning to sedate you at the wedding so you don't shame her by telling people that Dad once worked in the naval dockyards and you're only rich now because of a mesothelioma class action."

Penelope liked to pretend that she came from old money. She also told people that Dale was married to her job and avoided using the word "lesbian" around anyone she was trying to impress.

Ophelia said, "I got some papers for you, Dale, honey. Came last week."

Dale followed her to the writing desk in the alcove at one side of the fireplace. Ophelia opened the center drawer and stood a few feet away, hands on her hips, as Dale reached past the chocolate box to the space behind it. She pulled out a plain envelope that bore the Weitz & Luxenberg logo. The letter within informed Laurel that as per her instructions, the next settlement check of $127,000 would be forwarded directly to her daughter Mrs. Penelope Avaryss.

"Mrs. Avaryss come out here last week," Ophelia said. "She takes Miss Laurel in the bedroom to make private phone calls."

"Did you hear my mother talking?"

Ophelia laughed. "Miss Laurel just had her lunch. She sleeps in the afternoon. I guess Mrs. Avaryss might wake her up if she wanted her to say something."

Dale read the letter again and slipped it into her back pocket.

"Mrs. Avaryss had a realtor come see the house," Ophelia continued her disclosures. "You selling?"

"Not that I'm aware of."

Penelope had run the idea by Dale a few months ago. Even in the depressed real- estate market, Tarrytown properties were commanding big prices, especially genuine Victorians. Laurel had inherited the Porter family home from her parents not long after she was married. Dale had been brought up here, attending Sleepy Hollow High School and spending much of her childhood roaming the surrounding Rockefeller-owned parklands, hoping for a glimpse of the headless horseman. There wasn't much else to do.

Dale had flatly refused to talk to their mother about selling, and she thought Penelope had let go of the idea.

Ophelia said, "Your sister says it's time for Miss Laurel to move to assisted living."

Ophelia knew exactly what Dale thought about that possibility. They'd spoken recently about her mother's sudden deterioration. Alzheimer's crept up on some people and stampeded through the minds of others. Laurel was rapidly losing her memory but she loved her home, and Dale had no intention of uprooting her from the environment she'd known all her life.

She said, "When it gets bad, I'll move out here myself. You need to let me know when you think it's time, so I can make work arrangements."

Ophelia touched her arm. "You can stay put. We get by just fine."

Laurel called out, "Where did you put my red shoes?"

"They on your feet." Ophelia pointed.

Laurel stared down at the shoes like she'd never seen them before.

Dale said, "Finish your juice, Mom." If she was left alone, she forgot to eat or drink.

"You stole my car." Laurel glared at her.

Ophelia strode across the room and clamped a hand on Laurel's shoulder. "We're not going to talk any more about that car, Miss Laurel. You know where it is and how it got there."

"She took it." Laurel stabbed the air with both forefingers, aiming her wrath at Dale.

"You smashed that car into the gates all by yourself," Ophelia said patiently. "And Dale come rushing out here to go to the hospital with you. Then the tow truck took your car away. I watched with my own two eyes."

Laurel fell silent for a few seconds, digesting this information with a suspicious frown. "You're not my daughter," she informed Dale eventually. "My daughter is beautiful."

"Don't you mind her." Ophelia looked pained. "That's the disease talking."

"I know." Dale planted a kiss on Ophelia's ample cheek.

Their families had been under the same roof for almost thirty-five years, and Dale regularly thanked God for that fact. Ophelia's husband had been horribly injured in an accident at a site where Dale's dad was a construction engineer. The Porters took him and his family in when they lost their home, giving them a wing of the Tarrytown house that had originally been converted into an apartment for Laurel's mother late in life. The arrangement was supposed to be temporary, but when Dale was born as an afterthought, and Laurel was too depressed to cope, Ophelia took over caring for the family. She stayed on even after her son Jermaine joined the marines and Penelope, then Dale, left for college. She nursed her own husband until he passed, then Dale's dad as he slowly succumbed to the misery of his lung cancer.

"You staying for supper?" Ophelia asked.

"No, I'm working tonight."

"That's fine. I already fixed you some chicken for the drive back."

"I wish you wouldn't bother with that," Dale said. "You have enough to do."

She felt guilty every time she drove off, leaving Ophelia with the increasingly difficult task of caring for Laurel. Ophelia wasn't getting any younger, and Dale thought it was time she and Penelope took more of the burden. She wanted to have a conversation with her sister, the one Penelope kept avoiding.

"I thought if I did some extra shifts, I could take a leave and come stay out here," Dale said. "Then you can go visit with Jermaine and see the new baby."

Ophelia high-fived her. "He got a purple heart this time. I tell you that?"

"Jermaine's a genuine hero," Dale said. "You must be so proud."

"I wish his daddy was here."

"And mine," Dale said.

"God rest their souls." Ophelia lifted her gaze toward the ceiling as she always did when addressing the deity. Her air was one of expectancy, as if an answer was imminent. When God kept his opinion to himself, she focused on Dale once more. "Damn, I almost forgot. Last time Mrs. Avaryss was here she made a big old mess in Miss Laurel's room. I like to fell out."

"What do you mean?"

Ophelia's face was as serious as it ever got. "Your momma didn't raise no fool."

"She was looking for something?" Dale concluded.

With a shrug, Ophelia straightened the pillows behind Laurel and bent low to check her breathing. "She sure asked a lot of questions about that lockbox at the bank."

"What did you tell her?"

With a wicked sparkle in her eyes, Ophelia swung her hips and replied in a sing-song parody, "Miz Avaryss, I don't know nothing 'bout no lockbox. I just dumb ole Ophelia that cooks and cleans fo your momma."

"Uh-huh." Dale grinned.

"She wants the title papers for this house," Ophelia said dourly. "That's what I think."

Dale didn't reply. She was all out of excuses for her sister's strange behavior. The truth was, Penelope had done nothing but find fault with their mother ever since the settlement was reached. Laurel was to receive three million dollars in compensation over several years. Dale was thrilled about the financial security and incredibly relieved, given the ever-increasing cost of Laurel's care. Penelope, however, was steamed.

It made no sense, but Dale had learned one important lesson investigating homicides within families: money changes everything.

CHAPTER FIVE

"I wish you could have brought her down to the station house," Dale said as she and Sandy Smith climbed the narrow staircase to the third floor of a yet-to-be-gentrified walk-up just off W. 125th St.

"It's better this way. She doesn't want to leave the apartment."

"We could get her evaluated by the shrink if she would come in and make a statement." From what Dale had heard on the phone, Sandy's friend needed professional help.

Dale was surprised that they'd never been introduced. She and Sandy had met professionally when Sandy joined the District Attorney's office a few years ago. They often had a drink together after a long interview or a trial. Dale could recall mention of Giselle's name and vague plans that they would all go out sometime, but the date hadn't transpired.

"She's not crazy," Sandy said. "She's just making some bad decisions."

The stairs opened to a dimly lit hallway. Dale hoped they would reach the apartment before the pungent carpet fumes had time to suffocate them. Their destination was a door painted like one of those scenes in a travel magazine. A door within the door beckoned visitors into a terracotta-paved garden with views over what Dale took for a vineyard. This was Tuscany, or at least what she'd always thought Tuscany must look like.

Sandy rang the bell then stuck a key in the lock. "I keep a spare. Her mom always loses them."

"Does the mom live here, too?"

"Nashleigh Whittaker? No way. She's a celebrity fitness instructor. You've probably seen her on *The View*. She's got her own elders' workout show on cable, videos, books. The works. She's huge."

Dale looked around. "And her daughter lives *here*?"

"You don't want to know." Sandy made a face. "There's some history."

She pushed the door open and Dale followed her into a plain room with a high ceiling, wood floor, and naked brick walls. A few paintings decorated these. They looked like real art, not posters. A vase of wilted flowers occupied a simple wooden table. Parked to one side, in a rattan armchair crammed with faded velvet pillows, a young woman sat with a blanket-covered bundle in her arms.

Sandy rushed over and planted a kiss on her cheek. "This is the detective I told you about. Dale Porter from the 28th Precinct. Meet Giselle Truelove."

The name. You'd think the parents would have done something about it. But no. They'd sent their offspring out into the world to be mocked her entire life. She had that appearance, too, like a creature that got kicked a lot but still hoped for a tender touch.

Giselle looked Dale up and down like she was a child trafficker. "Show me some ID."

Dale offered her badge. "I'm a homicide detective, Ms. Truelove. I'm off duty this evening."

A veil of silky-straight dark copper hair swung forward as Giselle lowered her head to study the badge. "I've never seen one of these, close-up," she said in a respectful tone. She made no move to hand over the baby.

Dale offered the appropriate cue. "I can promise you, the infant you're surrendering will be well cared for."

Doe eyes. Now Dale knew where that description came

from. Giselle Truelove slapped her with a wounded stare straight out of *Bambi*. Here, for every schmuck who had ever found one floating in his beer, was the reason false eyelashes took off. Women wanted that melting, heavy-lidded gaze, those eyes with their velvet depths and mysterious emotions. Giselle seemed to blink more slowly than most people, or maybe that was an illusion caused by the lazy sweep of her eyelashes. Dale wondered how she made her living. She could be a makeup model in a magazine except for the scar that deformed her upper lip. Dale avoided looking at it. She didn't want to spook her.

"I've had a bad week," Giselle said. "I meant to take her to the hospital sooner, but I didn't feel like going out."

"No problem. I'm here to take care of all that for you."

Giselle smiled cagily. "Thank you for taking time out of your schedule. I know you must be very busy solving murders."

Dale was struck by the husky quality of her voice. The low, throaty range didn't quite fit her girlish appearance, and she also had a faint lisp. Dale guessed she'd struggled to conceal the impediment; she pronounced her words more carefully than most people.

Like an animal trainer dealing with the unpredictable, Sandy closed in on her friend and offered a treat. "I brought your favorite. Chocolate-covered marshmallows."

Dale wondered if she was supposed to make her move while Giselle was distracted by the candy. She waited for the right moment. Giselle relaxed her grip and lowered the bundle. Dale should have grabbed the infant then, but she lost all concentration. Breasts did that to her, and these were perhaps the most perfect pair she had ever seen. She wanted to arrest them.

Giselle drew the sides of her shirt together, explaining, "Babies need skin contact. I think the feel of my breasts is a comfort."

Dale found that highly plausible. She took a measured pace forward and extended her arms. "You're doing the right thing. Rescuing this child was a public service."

"What's going to happen to her?" Giselle fretted, ignoring Dale's outstretched arms. "You hear so many horror stories. Stupid social workers ignoring abuse. Runaways. Child prostitutes. They all seem to come from foster homes."

Dale almost laughed. A white baby girl discarded like trash and rescued from a dumpster? The story would be front-page news. Rich, infertile couples from all over the country would be jamming the lines. Children's Services would find a nice, upper-middle-class family in a good neighborhood. The ecstatic new parents would spend the next twenty years making up for the baby's unfortunate beginnings.

"You've got nothing to worry about," she said with conviction. "Trust me, this infant will be adopted in the near future. Most throwaways find permanent homes very quickly."

Giselle hugged the baby more tightly. She looked appalled. "Throwaways?"

Dale was not accustomed to situations that did not involve a dead body and a room full of cops. Her carefully rehearsed condolences and diplomatic questions for next-of-kin did not apply in this scenario. "Bad choice of words. Sorry."

She glimpsed a pink, scrunched face and a smooth pate with a lick of fine black hair. Suddenly, she felt outraged. If the mother had been standing in front of her she would probably have lost her self-control and broken a few teeth. With New York State's safe haven law, there was no excuse for abandoning a newborn to die. If an unhappily pregnant single had any brains she could spend her pregnancy on easy street, paid for by a fancy private-adoption lawyer. Dale knew a lap dancer who scored a cruise in the Bahamas for postnatal mental-health care, and who had all her college fees paid to "reduce stress." Her unwanted pregnancy was the best thing that ever happened to her.

Wanting to affirm that Giselle would face no consequences for keeping the abandoned baby longer than she should have, Dale said, "In the state of New York a mother who wants to surrender her newborn can also hand it over to a responsible person. In this case, we can say you assumed that responsibility in the mother's absence. I don't have a problem with that."

Sandy translated. "She's saying you won't face any charges."

Giselle stood up. She was a head shorter than Dale and would have looked waiflike if not for the breasts and the distinct flare of hips below her narrow waist. Her eyes shone with unshed tears. Dale was surprised again by their dark soft brown, an unexpected shade for a woman with fair skin and hair that seemed naturally copper. Dale had encountered the rare combination before, processing crime scenes over the years, but she'd never been as fascinated as she was now.

"I just wanted to do something good." Giselle kissed the baby on each cheek and placed it in Dale's arms. "I thought it was meant to be."

Her expression was so bereft, Dale considered arranging a fake birth registration and heroically letting her keep the baby. The right words for the occasion still didn't leap to mind. That was the norm when it came to women and emotion. She lifted the baby against her shoulder with one arm and hoped it wouldn't spit up on her jacket. She was relieved that she didn't have to arrest Giselle, although she took a moment to dwell on the idea of patting her down and handcuffing her.

Balancing the unaccustomed shape and weight of the infant, she took a card from her breast pocket and pressed it into Giselle's hand. "If you want to know what's happening, or if you have any questions, call me."

Giselle nodded forlornly. "Do you want to take a bottle or two of milk? I have some spare in the fridge. It's breast milk. That's much better than baby formula."

Dale could not stop her gaze from dropping once more to the breasts filling out Giselle's shirt. Her immediate suspicion must have been obvious.

Blushing, Giselle said, "I'm not the mother. The milk isn't mine. You can check if you want."

Before Dale could take full advantage of this offer, Sandy explained, "Giselle has been obtaining expressed milk from a woman in the neighborhood who lost her own baby."

The formality of this statement made it clear that something illegal was probably going on around the breast-milk supply. Dale didn't want to know. The baby was starting to squirm and she wasn't looking forward to spending the next twenty minutes listening to it screaming in the car, so she said, "Sure, I'll take whatever you have left."

As Giselle headed for the kitchen, Dale leaned closer to Sandy. "She just got dumped by her girlfriend?"

"Uh-huh." Sandy didn't miss much. "And she's way too high maintenance for you."

Dale watched Giselle bend to take a recycled grocery bag from a drawer. Outlined in her close-fitting jeans, her butt seemed as firm as her breasts, and each tempting attribute looked like a perfect fit for Dale's cupped hands. She sighed.

Sandy said, "Stick to what you're good at."

"Which is?"

"Being single."

Dale pasted on her bland cop-face as Giselle approached with disposable diapers peeping from the bag. Setting the load down on a chair, she said, "Don't overheat the milk."

"I won't," Dale said.

To her shock, Giselle stepped in close, caught hold of her free hand, and lifted it to her mouth. She placed the tip of her tongue against Dale's wrist for a single tantalizing second and said, "It should feel like that."

Dale wanted to ask for a repeat demonstration. Her skin prickled where the moist residue dried. Her pulse accelerated and her nipples tightened. She pictured Giselle naked. Bad idea. Sandy's elbow landed in her ribs, confirming that she was completely transparent. Had Giselle also noticed her lapse into lust? No. She was too busy staring at the baby.

Oddly disheartened, Dale took the grocery bag and they all

walked to the door and stood there in awkward silence. Sandy pecked Dale's cheek and said a relieved "thank you." Giselle took the baby's hand and cupped it in her own. A tear dripped off the tip of her nose. She backed away and covered her face. Dale mumbled something official-sounding and escaped as fast as she could.

As the door closed after her, she heard Giselle say, "Before I die, I want to love someone, that's all. Real love. Love bigger than me."

CHAPTER SIX

W e need to talk," Dale said as soon as her older sister occupied the chair the waiter pulled out.

They were having lunch at one of the temporarily hip Upper West Side eateries Penelope kept track of in her BlackBerry. Dale hoped this place could get over itself enough to serve a portion that would last her until a late-night pizza break.

"I'm sorry to keep you, darling," Penelope said. "The traffic was hideous."

She ordered Pellegrino and the waiter asked Dale if she wanted another beer. She declined and told Penelope she had already ordered a starter. Not that it mattered. Penelope only pretended to eat. After the sparkling water was served and the waiter had taken their meal orders, Dale began their conversation the way she always did.

"You look good."

Penelope's yardstick of beauty was the scrawny, blank-faced zombies that tracked through Bergdorf's as if on a conveyer belt. Immobile brows, non-descript noses, the same teeth, the same streaked ash blond hair. Dale didn't envy her counterparts at the Midtown North precinct. Imagine chasing down a female suspect who fit that description.

Penelope took the compliment as her due. "Pat Wexler," she shared. "You have to wait six months, but she's worth it. And with the wedding coming up..."

Dale nodded like she too was contemplating dermabrasion and extra Botox for the occasion. She said, "I don't have a lot of time, so—"

"Wait." Penelope was on her feet. "I simply have to say hello to someone. I'll be right back." In a rapid whisper, she explained. "Baron Karan, the party planner. I want him to do our anniversary."

Without waiting for a response, she strolled off in the limber walk of a woman who only took her Manolos off for the Pilates class. She swept past the target table before pausing and pivoting to greet the party planner like she'd only just noticed him. They exchanged a few words, and then Penelope walked away as if headed for an entirely different destination. After a few minutes she reappeared at Dale's side from the opposite direction.

"Thank God," she declared as she took her seat. "Baron thinks he has an opening for early September."

"Isn't Wayne's wedding in October?" Dale thought two big occasions so close together might clash.

Penelope shrugged. "Many of the wedding guests will attend both, so the anniversary party will give people something to talk about. You could say it's a warm-up. I'm planning a very special evening."

Dale translated that to mean Penelope intended to upstage the wedding ahead of time. She said, "Mom's looking forward to the big day."

With a martyred air, Penelope said, "I think we both know Mother won't have the faintest clue whether she was there or not a day later."

"That's why photographs mean so much to her," Dale said. "She doesn't feel so lost if she has proof she was actually at family events."

A waiter deposited a plate of breaded asparagus on the table.

"Fried," Penelope noted.

Dale ate a couple of spears. They were surprisingly good. It was time to get to the point. "I was talking to Mom's attorney. He got a fax from Weitz & Luxenberg about another payment, but it hasn't shown up yet."

"I'm dealing with it," Penelope said breezily. "Mom lost one a while ago. Did you know that? I had to have them issue another check. Three hundred thousand dollars. She probably threw it in the trash."

"Ophelia has instructions about the mail," Dale said.

"You can't expect a housekeeper to handle our mother's private financial affairs. That's asking for trouble."

"She's not *handling* Mom's affairs. I asked her to sort the mail and set aside any envelopes from the attorneys so she can pass them on to one of us."

"She hasn't passed anything on to me." Penelope sounded miffed.

"You've only visited Mom three times since Christmas."

"What's your point? That I don't do my bit?"

"All I'm saying is if I'm there every week doing the yard, I'll probably get the letters Ophelia sets aside."

"Fine," Penelope snapped. "You're a saint."

"So the payment that's just been sent?" Dale prompted. "What's the deal?"

"After my last visit with Mom, I thought it was wise to have them send it to me instead." Penelope ran bony fingers through her finely streaked hair, teasing it out a little. "Perhaps you haven't noticed the deterioration in her, seeing her all the time. But I was shocked."

"I notice how she is," Dale said.

"Then give me credit for taking sensible precautions to safeguard her interests."

"You have my number. Why didn't you discuss this with me?"

"I intended to. Have you any idea how busy I am?"

"No." Dale could not imagine what it must be like to have no job, one son who was no longer at home, a husband who spent half his life traveling, a full-time housekeeper, and no hobbies other than shopping, Pilates, and personal grooming.

"You're so self-righteous," Penelope said. "You think a stay-at-home wife and mother has nothing to do."

Dale consumed the rest of the asparagus. She was probably going to be landed with the check; she might as well eat what she was paying for.

"You can't even guess at the planning it takes to entertain every week," Penelope continued the chronicle of her stressful life. "To maintain the kind of contacts that matter. With the real-estate downturn, business has been slow for Carl this year, so networking is crucial."

Dale interpreted this doublespeak as best she could. "Are you saying money is tight?"

Penelope dismissed this notion with a tinkling laugh. "Everything is relative at our level. We've had better years, but it's never entirely predictable. One big deal and the situation resolves itself."

"What situation?"

"The cash-flow situation." Penelope heaved a sigh. "Really, Dale. It's none of your business. Everything's fine, but with the wedding and the anniversary party, we have some extra pressure this year, that's all. Between you and me, the timing sucks."

Dale studied her sister closely. The hands always gave her away. She had one bundled inside the other to prevent it from moving. As a kid, she'd always covered her mouth after a lie. As an adult, she'd learned to suppress the habit by keeping both hands down at all times.

"Penelope, you're talking to a detective," Dale said very softly. "I've known you my whole life. Do you think I can't see through your bullshit?"

Penelope gulped down some water. "Alright, so it's not that simple. For God's sake keep it to yourself. Don't tell Mom."

"What were you planning to do? Borrow the hundred and

twenty-seven thousand without telling her? Without telling *me*?"

"Of course not." A frown grappled with the inertia of Penelope's brow, tugging at her temples and hairline instead. "But it would certainly help." The plea in her tone was unmistakable. "Besides, it's rightfully our money. Why shouldn't we have the use of it now?"

"Mom's not dead," Dale said coldly.

Their father had left each of them fifty thousand dollars. The rest of his estate went to their mother. Penelope had spent her inheritance on a pearl necklace. Dale bought Google shares, sold them at a fat profit, and paid off part of her mortgage with the proceeds.

"She's a selfish old woman who was never there for either of us, or for Dad." Rage shook Penelope's voice yet the decibels remained at a quiet constant. "Now, she needs us and there you are running around after her like a puppy dog. Do you think she gives a damn what you want or who you are? She despises you because you never married. She thinks you're a failure as a woman."

Dale did not react. She'd always found it ironic that Penelope detested their mother, yet Laurel thought the sun shone out of her older daughter's butt. Dale was strictly second-best in her mother's eyes, but she knew Laurel was proud of her for being a detective, even if she didn't approve of women who chose a career instead of a husband. Yet Laurel had accepted her lesbianism without fuss. Penelope was not nearly as open-minded, and Dale strongly suspected the sentiments she was now attributing to their mother were actually her own.

"This is not about Mom," she said. "This is about you being in some kind of financial mess. How bad is it? And don't bother lying. I know how to get information."

Her sister barked a bitter laugh. "Where to start? Let me see. Carl hasn't filed a tax return in six years and the IRS is breathing down our necks. We need to sell the house but the market is soft, so we're overextended. We'll be lucky if the sale covers the mortgage. Shall I go on? Basically, my husband has been an idiot."

Dale could hardly process what she was hearing. "You sure had me fooled. I thought you and Carl were wealthy."

"We were until he decided to play golf instead of working. That five million he inherited when his dad died…it's all gone. Every last cent."

Dale tried to understand how anyone could blow five million bucks and not even have their house paid off. Clearly it was nuts for her sister to borrow money to prop up a lifestyle she and Carl couldn't afford in the first place. How would they ever get themselves into a secure position if they kept spending money they didn't have? Struggling to find the right words, she opted for a sympathetic note. "I'm really sorry. This must be very stressful."

Penelope clutched her hand, plainly fighting back tears. "I was worried you wouldn't understand. You've no idea how betrayed I feel. I've sacrificed everything for my family. I thought we had investments. I thought the house was mortgage-free. Now I discover Carl's been using it for credit." Spitefully, she added, "If he was worth anything at all, I'd divorce him tomorrow."

Dale wiped her mouth with the napkin, stunned by her sister's sense of entitlement. Penelope had never worked a day in her life or made any direct financial contribution to her marriage. She expected to live like a princess and her husband had made it happen, evidently without regard to the consequences. Now that she'd found out they could not afford the luxuries she took for granted, she was talking like their marriage was over. Dale felt like they were from different planets.

Their meals finally arrived. Penelope had ordered a salad. Dale's steak was perched on a stingy dollop of mashed potatoes. A few vegetables were arranged artfully around the edge of the plate. The meal looked like a child's portion. Dale cut into the steak and told the waiter it was fine. She usually bought a burger after she ate with Penelope, anyway.

For a short while, they consumed their food in silence. Dale took advantage of the lull to assemble her thoughts. "I think it's time to make some changes," she said as gently as she could. Penelope had to face reality but she wasn't going to like it. Dale started with an easy option. "There can't be much to do around the house anymore. Why spend three hundred dollars a week on a housekeeper you don't need?"

"Why indeed?" Penelope said with disdain. "I could just take out a front-page advertisement in *The New York Times* and announce that we're broke." In case her meaning was lost on Dale, she added, "One does not let the housekeeper go. It sends the wrong signal."

"To the people you need to impress?"

"When you move in certain circles there's an understanding that you...belong."

"You're living beyond your means." Dale tried for the voice of reason. "And you can't afford to do that anymore. It's time to get real."

Penelope looked at her like she had lost her mind. "Do you have any idea what you're saying?"

"I'm saying that it's over, and no amount of denial is going to make the IRS go away." She watched Penelope push her food around her plate and lost her temper. "For Chrissakes eat something so your brain will work."

Around them the conversation died away. Penelope's mouth dropped open. Waiters stared. Dale chewed what was left of her pitiful steak and tried to figure out when Penelope had lost sight of everything that truly mattered in life. With twelve years between them, they had never been close, but Dale had looked up to her big sister for most of her childhood. Penelope's princess complex was a family joke, and more often than not everyone indulged her. Tacitly, they'd all enabled her to behave the way she did, cushioning her from reality whenever it threatened to impact.

Dale wondered what their mother would have done, before her illness, if she knew Penelope's glamorous lifestyle was crumbling around her. To some extent, Laurel lived vicariously through Penelope; Dale had recognized that fact a long time ago. From high-school prom queen to bride, to young mother with a nanny and a country-club lifestyle, a big house, a successful husband. Expensive cars, first-class travel, luxury clothing. Laurel loved boasting about Penelope's perfect life. Dale could remember her gushing about the makeup cabinet in Penelope's bathroom. For some reason she thought her daughter had truly "made it" because she spent thirty dollars on every bottle of nail polish she owned, buying Chanel instead of Revlon. Penelope had a whole drawer of colors, at least thirty bottles.

Dale could think of better ways to spend a spare thousand bucks you could throw away on over-priced cosmetics, such as donating it to the Humane Society. But Penelope had different priorities and Dale tried not to judge her. She didn't know what her sister was compensating for, but apparently she could never be satisfied and she did not know how to stop herself.

"You could get a job," Dale suggested. If Penelope had to earn her own money like the rest of the world, maybe she'd think twice about how she spent it.

Predictably, her sister found that idea out of the question. "What could I possibly do? I'm not trained for anything."

"It's not too late to go to school. Lots of women get back into the workforce once their kids have left home."

Penelope sipped water like she had a bad taste in her mouth. "I just don't think that's *me*. And I'm not sure how I would find the time for a nine-to-five job."

Dale persevered. "You and Carl need to make a plan. If you sell everything and clear your debts, you can make some kind of arrangement with the IRS to pay what you owe, and maybe rent a small place until you get back on your feet."

Aghast, Penelope echoed, *"Rent a small place?* Are you insane?"

"No, but you're sure sounding that way," Dale said sternly. "You're sitting here telling me that you and Carl are virtually bankrupt, but you're rushing up to some high-priced party planner all set to spend a pile of money for your anniversary. Get real."

Penelope's bright blue eyes glittered with fury. "You get real, Dale. Our mother has millions in the bank and she's rattling around in that huge house on acres of prime real estate. Carl spoke to a developer. We could get at least two million for the property, and that's after closing costs. Wait!" She objected when Dale tried to interrupt. "Let me finish."

"I'm listening." Dale could not believe what she was hearing, but after a decade of phony conversations that meant nothing, her sister was finally speaking her mind. The least she could do was hear her out.

"I read about Alzheimer's," Penelope said like a student who'd done difficult homework. "My estimate is that Mom's probably got about four or five years left. If we set aside a few hundred thousand for her expenses in assisted living and split everything else, we'd have over two million dollars each."

Her shoulders dropped a little as if she had just relaxed. Did she think Dale would be elated by this information and immediately agree that they should dispatch their mother to a nursing facility and divide her assets before she died? Dale signaled the waiter for the check and thought about what she needed to say.

Penelope turned the conversation to meaningless chitchat about the wedding and the divine dinner set Wayne had chosen for the gift registry, the respective merits of possible honeymoon destinations, and the frightening vulgarity of the cake Elaine van Label had her heart set on. Dale signed the credit-card slip and took several deep breaths. After this, there would be no going back. She and Penelope would be enemies.

Slowly and succinctly, she delivered the response to her sister's proposal. "Penelope, we are not selling the Tarrytown house. And if you help yourself to a cent of Mom's money without my written agreement, I'll personally place you under arrest."

❖

Giselle set aside her palette and brushes and took a few paces back from her canvas. The painting was now four days old, just slightly younger than Vita. It was a week tonight that Giselle had saved her. Everything happened for a reason; wasn't that the cliché people invoked when explanations fell short?

Loving Vita as she did, so quickly and irrationally, made her wonder about her own mother. Had Nashleigh loved her that way, too? Had she fallen into enchantment, content to sit for hours staring down at the sleeping creature in her arms? Had she marveled at the perfection of fingernails like tiny shells and little feet so sensitive a kiss made them curl?

Giselle wrapped her arms around herself, acutely aware of a barrenness she'd never known before. She missed the warm heaviness of a baby in her arms, a head nestled against her breast. Before Vita, she would not have believed she could feel this way. She yearned to see the baby again, to hold her and kiss her and make sure she was warm and safe and well. Unable to relax, she rose and paced aimlessly around the apartment.

She thought about going downstairs and knocking on Dr. Redman's door, but she wasn't in the mood for another postmortem about the foolish risks she'd taken keeping Vita, the fact that she'd allowed herself to love what she knew she would lose. Giselle leaned against the kitchen counter and stared at the fridge door where Detective Dale Porter's card was parked beneath a retro magnet that featured a tame-looking woman with a beehive hairdo. The slogan read, "Her greatest regret was not having more sex."

Giselle removed the card and poked it under a more innocuous magnet. She had briefly suspected Sandy of trying to matchmake, and had made a comment or two about this possibility. But Sandy's denials seemed genuine; in fact she'd been pretty emphatic about Dale being the wrong type and a confirmed single with a job that didn't leave room for a girlfriend. Yes, the detective was good-looking and decent, but Sandy thought Giselle's next girlfriend should be the artistic type, someone who could bond with her over shared interests.

Besides, Dale had a "type" and Giselle wasn't even close. As far as Sandy knew, Dale went for sexy blondes who were usually cheating on partners. She always dumped them when she found out, but for a detective she seemed to overlook really obvious clues. Sandy suspected her of unconsciously choosing women who would not commit. She said Giselle deserved better and should save her emotional energy for Ms. Right.

Giselle opened the fridge and explored the contents halfheartedly. She didn't feel like eating, and most of the plastic-covered leftovers were probably well past their use-by dates. That was the problem with one-person eating. You could never finish a whole meal, so you were always stuck with semi-portions of this and that. Giselle could not afford to throw perfectly good food away, so she had absurd meals several times a week. Tonight's prospect was half a chicken-and-green-chili burrito, with Chinese shrimp and broccoli, and a slice of pizza.

She checked the wall clock and pictured Vita sleeping contentedly after her five o'clock feed. After Dale Porter left that evening, Giselle had been infuriated with herself. She should have gone to the police station with her. She should have insisted on seeing the social worker and requesting that she continue to foster Vita. Now it was too late. Vita was in the system, placed with an anonymous couple until her adoption. Sandy said the records would be closed and the best she could do was obtain a general answer about the adoptive family.

Giselle closed the fridge and took Dale's card down again. The detective had told her she could call, if she had any concerns. She'd thought about doing so, but had put it off, trying to let some time pass so she was less emotional. She thought if she waited, she would simply let go and accept that Vita was fine and would have a good life with parents who really wanted her, like most adopted children. So far, peace of mind had eluded her.

Telling herself it was only natural to need some reassurance, Giselle picked up the phone and dialed the detective's number. She expected to get a machine and was disconcerted when Dale Porter's warm, deep voice greeted her but did not invite her to leave a message.

When she failed to respond, Dale asked, "Who am I talking to?"

"Detective Porter, hello. It's Giselle Truelove, the woman with the baby you—"

"Yes, I remember." She sounded faintly amused. "What can I do for you?"

The question came across more like an invitation. Startled, Giselle remembered the feel of the detective's eyes on her, the fleeting taste of her skin, the lingering fragrance that did not belong to Sandy.

"Giselle?"

"I was just thinking about Vita…the baby, and I thought you might know how she's doing."

"I apologize for not phoning you sooner. It's been hectic."

"I don't mean to bother you. I just—"

"You're not bothering me," Dale said. "Far from it. If I wasn't talking to you, I'd be stuck in a confined space with a creep who took his last shower about five years ago, and that's from this week's highlight reel."

She actually sounded nervous, although that didn't seem likely. No doubt she was busy and trying to make idle conversation so Giselle would feel at ease. Giselle obliged with some quiet laughter.

"If it's a bad time, I could call back later."

"There's never a good time." Dale paused. "I have an idea. How about I swing by your apartment after I get off duty? That way I can call the social worker this afternoon and get the latest."

"Really, you don't mind doing that?"

"My pleasure."

Giselle heard someone talking in the background and Dale said she had to go.

"What time should I expect you?" Giselle asked hastily.

"Let's say six, in case I'm delayed."

Before Giselle could ask if she wanted to have supper, the phone reverted to dial tone. Giselle thought she'd probably been saved by the bell. It would have been embarrassing if she'd offered and Dale declined with some weak excuse.

CHAPTER SEVEN

S ix shootings in one day. How often do we see that anymore?" said Babineaux, always nostalgic for the adrenaline-charged shifts of the early 1990s.

The citywide homicide rate was at dizzying heights before Mayor Giuliani's zero-tolerance policy. Shoot-outs between Dominican drug dealers and local gangs ensured every detective had a full caseload, if the usual muggings, rapes, and family violence were not enough.

"Who's catching?" the lieutenant yelled.

"We got it, sir." Dale stood.

"We're up twenty percent," Babineaux pronounced as they took the stairs.

"I wouldn't get excited," Dale said. "There's a bunch of reclassified homicides in the latest numbers."

"Six shootings is not a blip on the radar."

Her partner could not hide his relief. The forty-year low in 2005 had most cops wondering if there was any future in making detective. Ambitious patrol officers were looking at other options these days, like the Joint Terrorism Task Force or even the private military sector. What was the point in taking the extra classes to specialize in homicide if your precinct could only report eight or ten suspicious deaths in a year? The CompStat process had resulted in redeployment of police resources all over the city. Even in Washington Heights, officers who had once spent most of their time processing crime scenes were now all about prevention, which was fine if giving talks at schools got your motor running.

"Guns, that's all they respect anymore. You do the math. Moron plus automatic weapon equals dead kid." Babineaux sighed. "Fucking fascinating it's not."

Back in the day, when the body count in Central Harlem was impressive, the range of murder weapons kept detectives guessing. Blunt-force trauma inflicted by a pumpkin. Suffocation with hamburger. Perpetrators used their imaginations. Not any more. Cause of injury or death was a gunshot wound or a knife wound. The typical killer was a young male who blamed anyone but himself for his choices. Dale had trouble with the excuse-making that went on around these offenders. As far as she was concerned, kids all over the world would be thrilled to exchange their miserable lives for the dilemmas faced by poor urban youth in New York City.

"You still thinking about the Cold Case Squad?" Babineaux asked.

"I've put out some feelers," Dale said.

The squad was one of the more interesting places for a homicide detective to work, and with almost nine thousand homicides unsolved from the past thirty years there was plenty of scope. Dale didn't like to think of that many killers roaming the streets, enjoying life, convinced they'd gotten away with murder.

"Beats writing tickets for arborcide." Babineaux was still getting over a recent incident in which a patrolman fined some poor schmuck $1000 for chaining his bicycle to a tree. Damaging city property was no joke, and a premeditated attack on a tree incurred special wrath.

Dale got in the driver's seat. "Where are we going?"

"The Apollo."

"Convenient." Dale checked her pager in case the social worker had returned her third phone call. She could get Babineaux to drop her off at Giselle's apartment after they were through.

"Hey, Marcia thinks I robbed a bank to buy that necklace," Babineaux said. "You didn't tell me it was from Tiffany's."

"You saw the box."

"Three thousand bucks. She looked it up on the Internet. Jazz, that's what they call the design."

Dale grimaced. Penelope could have spent a fraction of that amount for something Dale would have liked. But that would have required her having some idea who Dale was. The gift was not about her taste or her identity, she realized; it was strictly about impressing her.

"I'm glad Marcia's happy," she said. At least the necklace would be treasured by a woman who took nothing for granted.

"I feel bad," Babineaux confessed, plainly embarrassed. "You sure you don't want something for it, now you know what it's worth?"

"I guess you're not going to shut up about it until I agree," Dale said.

Babineaux guffawed, but there was a nervous edge to his laughter.

"I could use a new pocket knife. None of your cheap made-in-China crap. The best. Then we're even."

Babineaux nodded happily. "You got it."

❖

"Blood." Giselle gulped.

Dale inspected herself. "Damn."

"It's fine. It's nothing, really." The smear on her jacket and shirt wasn't that bad. Giselle wished she'd had the good manners not to mention it. "Come in, Detective."

"That's Dale, please." She hesitated. "I should go home and shower, and change. Simple precautions."

"And you hate being dirty," Giselle guessed.

"Yeah, I really do." Dale grinned. "How can you tell?"

"I'm not sure. Sometimes I just know things about people."

"You pick up details on an unconscious level." Dale's sleepy gray eyes combed her slowly up and down. "You could be a detective."

"Oh, no. I could never do your job." Giselle felt her skin warming under the frank scrutiny. "If you'd like to take a shower, you're very welcome. I can probably find a T-shirt you could wear. They're not all like this." She indicated the low-cut pastel green top she was wearing, a close-fitting style she'd chosen in an effort to look more interesting than she was.

In hindsight, she felt silly about agonizing over what to wear for Dale's visit. It wouldn't matter how tight her clothes were, or what she did with her boring dead-straight hair; she would never be mistaken for the sexy blonde Sandy said was Dale's type.

"That's really nice of you," Dale said. "I'd feel more comfortable not transporting half a crime scene around your home. Do you have a trash bag I can put my cleaning in?"

She took off her jacket and began to unbutton her shirtsleeves. Giselle was transfixed, collecting impressions so quickly her mind reeled. Dale was very attractive. Yes, very. And the right height. She took care of herself. Good shoulders. Tan. A mouth worth kissing. Short wheat-colored hair. Not a statement cut. Nothing to prove. Very clean. Her nails filed down. Hands square and a little chapped, like she scrubbed a lot.

Dale stopped undressing. "Forgive me. You can tell I spend too much time in a shared locker room." Great smile. Knee-buckling, in fact.

"Let me show you the bathroom." Giselle knew she was bright red. "I only have one. It's through my bedroom."

She wanted to hide her bed, so Dale wouldn't see the old teddy bear and the quilt that once belonged to Grandma Caldwell. A homicide detective was in her room, the room of a convicted murderess's granddaughter. Giselle gasped before she could stop herself. She covered her mouth. Dale was looking at her strangely.

"You can shower in here," Giselle mumbled. She pushed the bathroom door open too hard, and a loose hinge she been trying to fix finally severed its contact with the wood.

Dale grabbed the unsteady door and propped it back in the frame. "Don't worry. I can fix it. Do you have a drill and a screwdriver?"

"No, but my neighbor has tools." Slow down, Giselle thought in a panic. She could hear herself lisping. Controlling the movement of her tongue against her teeth, she said, "If you want to take your shower, I'll go ask him."

Again the smile. Giselle wished the far-too-attractive detective would stop looking at her that way. Standing here in the bedroom, just the two of them, made everything seem very intimate. Distracted, she glanced at the bed. Her mind promptly presented her with a tableau of flesh. Two women knotted in passion. The mental image made her heart grapple against the walls of her chest. She backed away from Dale, putting a safe distance between herself and the cause of her internal turmoil.

"Towels are on the high shelves." She felt breathless. "Please help yourself to some fresh soap."

Dale thanked her. With one hand propped against the door frame, she seemed completely at ease, as if *she* owned the room and Giselle was the stranger. They stared at each other.

Dale said, "I have good news about the baby."

The baby. Giselle started guiltily. From the moment Dale had arrived until right now, she hadn't thought of Vita at all. Was that the kind of mother she would have made—the kind who left her baby in a stroller outside a store, got distracted while shopping, and drove off without her?

"I figured you were probably bursting to ask and just being polite," Dale said, very calm and professional. "But I don't want to keep you on tenterhooks. She's doing fine. She's with a great foster family with two kids and a dog. These people are cream of the crop. Abandoned babies get extra attention from Children's

Services. They'll make sure she's just fine."

Giselle nodded. She was afraid to speak. When she got emotional her lisp was uncontrollable, and she knew how ridiculous she sounded. Forcing herself to breathe, and avoiding the letter "s," she said, "We can talk later. I'll go get what you need from my neighbor."

Dale's gaze slid over her, then flicked to the bed. Something in her expression changed, and after a long pause she asked, "Would you care to come to dinner with me?"

Giselle decided it was a good idea not to think too hard about her answer. She said, "Yes."

"Good. I'd like that." This time Dale cruised her so blatantly, Giselle could not pretend she was imagining it.

❖

Dale poured more wine into Giselle's glass. She didn't bother to ask herself: What am I thinking? Or: How many ways can Sandy Smith make my life hell?

She was past explaining herself to anyone. She wasn't a kid and neither was Giselle, despite the lisp, the nervous giggle, and the painfully obvious self-doubt. Her lack of confidence was, Dale conceded, the one roadblock that stood in the way of a tidy, mutually gratifying seduction. She generally avoided sleeping with vulnerable women. They got needy, and too much could go wrong. On the other hand, she knew enough to recognize the warning signs, and Giselle was not the pushy type. She would be easier to handle than some of Dale's devious, passive/aggressive exes.

Unless her powers of observation had failed her, Dale was pretty certain they were on the same page. She suspected Giselle had been thinking about sleeping with her ever since that awkward conversation in the bedroom. One-night stands obviously weren't her usual MO; she seemed to miss most of Dale's double entendres. But she'd just been dumped by a cheating girlfriend, and in that situation women did things that were out of character. Dale was fine about taking full advantage. In her experience, rebound flings worked for both parties. They were uncomplicated, hot, and short-lived. Ideal, in other words.

The only trouble was, she could not quite read Giselle and kept wondering if she was simply being nice to the detective who could supply information about baby Jane Doe. Sometimes it seemed like she had no idea she was sending mixed signals, or how they might be interpreted. She was inexperienced, an astonishing state of affairs in New York City, but it seemed obvious that the scarred mouth and mild speech impediment loomed larger in her mind than in anyone else's. As a consequence she was shy. Dale was surprised to find this very appealing.

They were at the dessert stage.

Dale offered, "Want to share?"

Giselle shook her head. "I couldn't possibly, but you go ahead."

Dale asked for the check. When it arrived, Giselle insisted on a split. Dale didn't put up a fight. Making a casual date feel beholden was a bad move. They walked back to the apartment in the crisp spring air. Harlem smelled almost pleasant. Things had changed since the days when officers from the two-eight rounded up dealers, pimps, hookers, and panhandlers every night, and beat up suspects in the holding cells.

When they reached the Tuscany door, Giselle said, "I'll get your clothes."

Not the invitation she'd expected. Dale weighed her options and decided she had nothing to lose. "I hope that offer includes coffee."

"Oh. I was trying not to take any more of your time."

"Do I look like I want to escape?'

"No." With a shy smile, Giselle unlocked the apartment and led her in.

Dale flicked the light switch inside the door. It didn't work.

"Stay where you are or you'll fall over a table," Giselle warned. "I'll get the lamp."

A moment later, soft light pooled in a corner of the room. Dale didn't sit on the sofa, as Giselle suggested. She followed her to the kitchen and watched her make the coffee. Most women understood that "coffee" was a euphemism at times like this and they didn't need to go through the whole routine, but apparently Giselle had skipped the Dating 101 classes. Even worse, she had to conceal a yawn.

"Cream?"

"Just a little, thanks." Dale accepted her mug and dutifully sipped.

Giselle watched her with transparent unease. "I was wondering." The words came out in a rush. "Do you think I could see the baby?"

Great. They were going to have *this* conversation. "I'm afraid that's not possible," Dale said, mentally kissing good-bye to what might have been. "There's no way Children's Services will give out an address for her."

"Not even to you?"

"Not to anyone."

"It was worth a try." Giselle sounded dispirited. Her dark doe eyes drifted to an artist's easel and painting paraphernalia stacked against an internal wall.

"You paint?" Dumb question, Dale thought.

"Sometimes." The tone was dismissive. Apparently she kept her hobby to herself.

Dale wandered into the living room and took in the paintings scattered around the walls. They were an eclectic mix, mostly portraits. "Are any of these yours?"

"All of them."

Dale was impressed. The pictures spoke about their subjects in ways a photograph couldn't. "You're very gifted."

Giselle laughed. "Be careful. Flattery might result in an offer to give you one."

"Really? Which is your favorite?" Dale asked, aware that the question was probably impossible to answer. How could any artist hold one of their works dearer than another?

Giselle lifted a canvas that was facing the wall. "It's hard to paint from memory alone. The skin tones never seem quite right."

The unfinished work she turned toward Dale was arresting. The baby lay on her side, arms crossed so her hands nestled beneath her chin. The simple image would have been sweet and comforting, except for the baby's stare. Dale's heart almost stopped in her chest. Innocence. Betrayal. Accusation. Grief. The unfinished state of the painting only made the stare all the more direct and personal.

Unsettled, she said, "It's very good."

"Now you understand why I need to see her again."

"I'm sorry. I wish I could make it happen." Dale meant every word. She was surprised at herself, but she'd always been a sucker for damsels in distress, and Giselle was nothing if not damselish. Trying not to dwell overtly on her charms, Dale asked, "Do you sell your work?"

"I'm not good enough."

"Isn't that for the buyer to decide?"

"There are a lot of portrait painters with real credentials," Giselle said. "It's hard to break into that field without the right contacts."

"You've tried?"

"I don't think I'm ready. I'm still learning."

"Well, for what it's worth I'd buy one of your paintings," Dale said.

Smiling faintly, as if Dale had just paid her an undeserved but kindly compliment, Giselle set the painting down again, face to the wall. She stayed where she was, standing next to the easel, hands clasped loosely in front of her. "You could have told me about the baby over the phone."

"Yes."

"Why did you come here?"

"I'm not exactly sure," Dale said honestly. "I thought you were owed more than a phone call, I guess. You saved that baby's life."

"Thank you. It was very nice of you to bother. And thank you for your company. Dinner was fun."

A pleasant farewell, Dale thought. Disappointing, but not entirely unexpected. She set her coffee cup on the nearest table. "Perhaps we could do it again some time."

"Perhaps."

Giselle folded her arms beneath her spectacular breasts. She seemed to be at pains to avoid eye contact. Dale couldn't figure out if she was saying good-bye or just waiting for her to make a move. Most women sent a clear signal if they wanted her to take the upper hand.

"I cook a little," she said, wanting to drop a non-threatening hint. "Maybe I could tempt you into spending an evening at my place."

"Are you asking me on a date?"

"Yes."

Giselle finally lifted her gaze. Her small oval face scrunched slightly as if she was puzzled. "Did Sandy put you up to this?"

"No, I'm an opportunist." At the quizzical tilt of Giselle's head, Dale explained, "What can I say? I find you attractive."

Giselle's arms fell to her sides. Laughing softly, she abandoned the wall and drifted a few steps closer, her thin floral skirt gliding back and forth across her slender thighs. "I thought I was imagining it."

"No." Dale gave a self-effacing laugh. "I was being obvious."

"You know I just had a sordid breakup."

"Yes. I'm sorry if she hurt you."

Dale closed the gap a little more. They weren't close enough to touch, but she could smell Giselle's perfume. It was flowery, but a hint of ginger and citrus offset the sweetness. Her neck looked delectably soft.

"I suppose Sandy told you everything," Giselle said.

"She warned me to stay away from you."

Giselle's gaze traveled from Dale's mouth to her throat and continued down her body. "Same here. She said you only date sexy blondes."

"I wonder why that doesn't sound like a compliment?"

The melancholy left Giselle's eyes. With a teasing sparkle, she said, "I only date bitches who cheat on me."

"I hate to cramp your style, but I don't cheat."

"Do you dance?"

"Only as an excuse to hold a woman."

"Well, that's a start."

Dale wasn't sure exactly what they'd just negotiated, but Giselle seemed to think they were headed in the same direction. She stepped in closer and hooked her arm in Dale's.

"I'll walk you to the door," she said, leaving no doubt at all that kissing did not happen on a first date.

Dale was intrigued more than let down.

As they passed the kitchen, Giselle gathered up the trash bag. "Here's your crime scene."

Dale bundled the bag under one arm. She and Giselle stood in the open doorway smiling at each other for longer than they needed to. There was something romantic about that, she decided as she trudged down the stairs a few seconds later. Out in the street, she loitered in front of the crappy apartment building, unkissed and horny and gazing up at Giselle's front window. When she saw the curtain move, she waved and Giselle waved back.

That was also romantic, she thought.

❖

Giselle dropped the curtain and turned off the lamp. She didn't feel like watching TV or reading a book, and she avoided painting at night. Bad lighting made the effort counterproductive, and she would only have to revisit every detail the next morning. In a worst-case scenario the effects she was hoping for could be destroyed and she would have to scrape down to the dead underlayer or beyond, until she reached umbra, then start again. Sometimes she became completely disheartened and abandoned the painting entirely. If the imprimatura was compromised, she could never settle. Every additional layer only compounded the problems.

Portraits always started out in one dimension, a composition of edges, lighting, and value patterns that became the foundation for every subsequent brushstroke. Some people made their initial drawings very tight and detailed. Giselle preferred a looser, more organic approach that allowed her to change values and transitions as her sense of her subject developed.

When something went wrong, it didn't matter that other people probably wouldn't notice the error. They only saw what was on top. But she knew what was concealed beneath. If the underlayers were corrupted the painting became a mask to her, the finishing layers nothing more than a thin cosmetic veneer designed to disguise, not reveal. People were already cloaked in everyday life, constructing the facades that made them feel safe and comfortable. She didn't want to replicate the same process. She supposed that was why she painted portraits; she wanted to see more.

Painting Vita was very different from painting her other subjects. A baby was unaware of image. Nothing was hidden but its potential. A baby was naked and unself-conscious. Yet Giselle had the sense that Vita's portrait said more about *her* than it did about the baby. Oscar Wilde's comment jumped to mind: Every portrait that is painted with feeling is a portrait of the artist, not of the sitter.

Lack of time was a problem. She hadn't spent long enough with Vita to chart every subtle change in her expression. All she had was memory and a few photographs. She had learned from past experience that the more she depended upon those instead of a live sitter, the more her painting became a likeness instead of a portrait. She had more to say about Vita than that.

Disconcerted, she wandered to her bedroom, chewing on her upper lip, aware of her scar and the little knot of flesh that lay beneath. She took for granted that her mouth was different on each side. As she ran her tongue between her top teeth and her lip, she could feel the telltale evidence of her imperfection. It always worried her that others could feel it, too. She avoided kissing for that reason.

With Bobbi that had been easy. It wasn't rocket science to figure out that the flaw turned her off. Bobbi tensed up every time their mouths connected. By the time they'd been dating for a few months, they simply didn't go there. That was nothing new. None of Giselle's former girlfriends had ever been completely at ease kissing her. Either they worried about hurting her or unwittingly causing damage, or they were strangely obsessed with her mouth and wanted to take time out to discuss her surgeries at length. Or they were distracted by the sight, or the feel, or the thought, and lost focus.

Dale Porter wanted to kiss her. Giselle touched her lips and imagined the sensation. She wanted to kiss Dale, too, and almost had. But she dreaded the possibility that Dale might be repelled and lose interest. They didn't know each other at all. Maybe if they did, they would discover a connection and the physical side would be less important than it seemed. Giselle didn't want to blow all chance of finding out.

She'd thought about inviting Dale to spend the night, but if they were going to have sex, kissing was the usual starting place, and it was too soon for that hurdle. Even though they were virtual strangers, Dale struck Giselle as the sensual type. She would want to kiss and make out. That kind of woman was never satisfied with a sexual encounter focused solely on the mechanics of getting off. Giselle understood completely. She liked sensuality herself.

Normally she would never have sex on a first date, yet throughout her meal with Dale, the possibility had hovered like a silent third party at their table. Neither of them had acknowledged its presence. Dale talked about her job and mentioned her mother, who had Alzheimer's. Giselle rambled on about movies she liked and places she hoped to visit one day. They'd had some laughs. Dale was easy to be with. And distractingly hot.

Now that she was home alone, Giselle couldn't help but dwell on what could have been. She got undressed and showered mechanically, imagining Dale's hands on her body. Dale's mouth on her throat. What kind of lover would she be? Giselle's few girlfriends were all very feminine in appearance and mannerisms, the opposite of Dale. Giselle supposed in a job like police work, a tough exterior was essential. She wondered who Dale was, underneath, and why it even mattered to her. Chances were, if they dated they would soon find they were incompatible and move on. According to Sandy, Dale was "only roadworthy for the short haul." That was how she described women who could not commit to a long-term relationship.

True or not, Giselle didn't have a big problem with the idea. In fact, she was beginning to think it was time to try the short-haul approach herself. If she wasn't attempting to have the perfect LTR, maybe she wouldn't feel like such a failure every time she had a breakup. Despondently, she turned out the lights, flopped into bed, and lay on her back.

Yes, she would sleep with Dale if the opportunity arose. Why create roadblocks? Why agonize over the future? She could handle the situation if they dated again. She knew how to avoid awkward first kisses.

CHAPTER EIGHT

What's your dress size," Nashleigh asked.

"I can buy my own clothes, thank you," Giselle replied.

She had done her best for this special occasion, knowing her mother would choose a swanky place. They were at Daniel, an opulent French restaurant awash with neoclassical colonnades, red velvet drapery, and snooty waiters. This was where Nashleigh brought gorgeous young men to prove she was the one who wrote the checks. Everything on the menu involved truffles or morels. The place was nirvana if you lived to eat pig's feet.

Giselle shuffled around to get more comfortable on a tall red velvet chair that left her feet dangling slightly above the plush carpet. "This dress is Vivienne Westwood," she informed her mother. "I paid plenty for it."

"At the recycled designer store," Nashleigh murmured. "I know you."

Fabio kissed his fingertips. "*Bellissima*. She is almost as beautiful as her mamma."

Nashleigh patted his cheek. "You're so sweet." To Giselle, she said, "Where he comes from, no one understands a woman who doesn't make the most of herself."

Fabio endorsed this sentiment effusively. "Your mother, she is like Sophia Loren, no?"

The resemblance escaped Giselle, but she said, "Wow, you *are* madly in love with her."

Nashleigh gave her a look. "What was I saying? Oh, yes. Your dress size. Four?"

"Six up top," Giselle replied. "Four below."

Fabio looked bewildered.

Nashleigh informed him, "Giselle has oversized breasts for her dimensions and did not show up for the appointment I made to discuss a reduction."

"Call me crazy, but I decided to keep my nipples where they are," Giselle explained sweetly. "Instead of having them…you know…cut off and reattached in a different place after the breasts were downsized."

Fabio paled.

Returning to her train of thought, Nashleigh said, "I have several designs to show you. They all minimize the bust."

"Designs for what?"

"Your bridesmaid's dress."

"No." Giselle covered her ears and shook her head. "Absolutely not."

Nashleigh pulled Giselle's hands away and firmly placed them on the table. "You're my daughter. This is my wedding."

"Been there, done that. Remember last time. Four hundred people, and I had to march down the aisle wearing a see-through dress and a *bonnet*."

"We were doing the Empire period," Nashleigh protested. "And that dress wasn't see-through. It was opaque, and only because the fabric had to be damp."

"My *nipples* showed."

Nashleigh got righteous. "No one complained."

"You have people sucking up to you all the time," Giselle said disdainfully. "Pick one of *them*. Or hire a model, so you don't need to be embarrassed by my figure."

Nashleigh assumed an air of wounded dignity. "I have only one daughter. Your figure doesn't matter. No one will be looking at you, they'll be looking at me."

Fabio seized Nashleigh's hand. His dark eyes flashed at

Giselle, brimming with Italian emotion. "Is this such a big thing, that your mamma asks? She gave you life."

"Oh, God." Giselle laid her forehead in her hands. Defeat was inevitable. Now was probably the best opportunity she would ever have to negotiate terms she could live with. She got herself together and announced her opening position. "This time I see the dress and approve it. I choose the fabric. I try it on *before* the day. I do not wear a hat or any other stupid thing on my head. Try something unexpected, and I'll walk down the aisle in *jeans*."

Nashleigh produced a leather folder from beneath the table, slapped it open, and smugly challenged, "Criticize these, missy."

Three designs were sketched out and samples of fabric were attached in a little booklet. Each dress was stunning. Amazed, Giselle asked, "Who designed these?"

"Let's just say I'm hoping for a hint of originality, so we are *not* wearing Vera Wang." Nashleigh and Fabio took a moment to kiss each other's hands. After they'd wiped themselves off on their napkins, Nashleigh asked, "Well? What do you think?"

Giselle's throat closed. This had to be the first time in her life that her mother had noticed what she really looked like and suggested clothing that would flatter her. The models in the sketches had her small waist and full breasts, and even her straight copper hair down to their shoulders. The dresses flowed across their bodies as if they were created with dance in mind.

Flabbergasted and truly touched, she said, "These are perfect for me, Mom. I'd be happy with any of them. Why don't you choose?"

Nashleigh broke into a radiant plum-tinted smile and draped her arm around Fabio. "She loves them."

"*Si.* We have success."

It dawned on Giselle then that Fabio had lent something to the equation that had been missing in the past. He had brought a sense of her to Nashleigh's choice of design. She couldn't get angry that Nashleigh hadn't arrived at the ideal decisions all by herself, without outside input. Her mother had never seen her as anything but a little girl with a facial deformity and a speech defect.

Giselle had been operated on as an infant, and after progressive surgeries and orthodontic treatment through her childhood, she had been left with nothing but a slight scar. The shyness Nashleigh despised was less about her lip and more about her speech problems. Giselle had grown up avoiding people so she would not have to embarrass herself in interactions. Even now, despite years of speech therapy, she felt uncomfortable in social situations.

Nashleigh thought the answer was more exposure and perhaps she had a point, but Giselle was not an extrovert. She didn't want to be the center of attention, as her mother did. Nashleigh's efforts to thrust her into a social life only made her want to hide. She knew this tendency frustrated her mother, so she made a big effort for any important occasions Nashleigh wanted her to attend. She would have to go to the latest wedding, regardless, but this time she would not be publicly humiliated.

Raising her champagne glass, gratified at her own small triumph, she said, "To Nashleigh and Fabio, and a beautiful wedding day."

They sipped, and Nashleigh entered into serious discussion with the sommelier about the right wines to have with their meals. As the two weighed the merits of various costly vintages, Fabio leaned toward Giselle and drew a photograph from his breast pocket.

"My brother Lorenzo." He placed the photo on the heavy white tablecloth. "Very handsome, no?"

"Yes. Quite the gene pool, your family."

Pleased with himself, Fabio confided, "I tell him of your beauty. Your *innocence*."

Nashleigh adjusted her décolletage and joined the conversation. "Lorenzo is going to be the best man, so he'll be partnering you."

Giselle wondered how she was going to wiggle out of entertaining this hunk for the duration of the wedding. She would be there alone, demonstrably in need of conversion to heterosexuality. Clearly this responsibility weighed heavily upon Fabio. His candidate for the seduction duties would tempt a nun.

"My brother, he is also a very good dancer."

"There's nothing like a European man." Nashleigh sighed. "So virile."

She and Fabio exchanged a long, smoldering look.

Giselle said, "I'll be delighted to meet your family, Fabio. I wish I could speak your language but I've only been to Italy twice. I loved it. Especially Tuscany."

Nashleigh's face glowed with delight that seemed genuine. Grabbing Giselle's arm she said, "You're going to love our other big news, pudding."

Giselle instantly rejected the first thought that crossed her mind. Her mother couldn't possibly be pregnant. She looked only thirty-five, but her ovaries were twenty years older than that. All the same, Giselle stole a quick look at her stomach.

Nashleigh pounced instantly, giggling and whispering in Fabio's ear.

He said, with a mournful air, "Ah, I wish it were so."

"Me, too, my darling." Nashleigh teared up convincingly. "To carry your child. Nothing could make me happier."

They cupped each other's faces.

Giselle groaned. "What big news are you talking about?"

"The wedding." Nashleigh managed to keep her hands to herself for long enough to extract a tourist brochure from her purse. It featured images of a rustic church and strapping, barefoot villagers dancing in a barrel of grapes. "We've decided to have it in Tuscany. Just close friends and family."

"A real Italian wedding." Fabio flashed his teeth. "My relatives will come from Verona."

Giselle could not process the information. Nashleigh's last wedding was a media spectacle, packed with minor celebrities, hangers-on, has-beens, and wannabes. The event had received an inside spread in *People* magazine. How would Nashleigh live if she didn't get the cover this time?

"What about all the usual guests?" Giselle ventured.

Nashleigh shrugged like she hadn't given much thought to the American end of things. "We can have a reception here later in the year, after the honeymoon."

"Tuscany," Giselle repeated blankly.

"I thought you'd be pleased." Nashleigh sounded piqued. "A small, intimate event. Not too many people."

"I am," Giselle said hastily. "I guess I'm surprised. I thought you'd want something more…visible."

"I've had the big marquee wedding. It didn't make me any happier. And this is for Fabio, too. Most of his family wouldn't be comfortable with air travel."

Nashleigh was forswearing a huge, glittering publicity fest for the sake of a down-home party with a bunch of Italian farmers. Giselle was lost for words. The waiter took their meal orders with the calm fortitude of a man accustomed to serving his inferiors. Giselle chose the first entrée that didn't scare her.

While they waited for the appetizers to arrive, she came up with a wild idea, a surefire way to escape the agenda of Fabio's handsome brother. All she had to do was soften her mother up before she asked the requisite favor. Heartened, she launched into fulsome praise. "Tuscany is a fantastic idea. All the classy people are choosing intimate weddings these days. That's a statement. Intelligent people find crass displays of wealth offensive in a world with so much poverty."

Nashleigh soaked up the positive feedback. "You know, after the last million-dollar wedding I went to, I said to myself, 'This time, keep it simple.' It's so easy to lose sight of what the occasion is really about, two people pledging their lives to one another."

"Exactly." Giselle clasped both hands over her heart. "I can see how much you and Fabio love each other. You look like a teenager, Mom."

Nashleigh fluttered. Fabio leaned over and kissed Giselle delicately on the forehead like she was a little girl. She was on a roll. Reminding Nashleigh of her good-mother credentials, she said, "By the way, thanks for the check, Mom. It's been a big help."

"You're welcome, pudding. Everything I have is yours. You know that, don't you?"

"I don't like to take you for granted." It was the truth. "You're very generous, but I want to make it on my own just like you did. You're my role model, Mom."

Again, not a complete lie. Giselle admired her mother's determination and hard work. She could have just divorced a couple of men and lived off alimony. Instead she'd made her own way in the world and earned her success.

Nashleigh's hazel eyes narrowed and she subjected Giselle to a suspicious stare.

"Is there something you want? I told you I would get you a car. You can have anything. Not a Ferrari or a Porsche. You couldn't handle them."

Giselle shrugged. "I don't want a car. I'm just happy for you. It's so good to see you with a man who truly appreciates you instead of those assholes who never knew the value of what they had."

Nashleigh had something to add to this theme. "Your father. Jerk of the Millennium."

To Fabio, Giselle recounted the story she had heard so frequently over the years. "This woman gave up everything to sit by my bedside night and day during my surgeries. She scrimped so I could have the best orthodontist money could buy. My father didn't contribute a dime."

Fabio proposed another toast, which prompted the sommelier to dispatch an underling to replenish their champagne and present them with a new bottle.

"To Nashleigh." Fabio gazed adoringly into his future-wife's eyes. "A beautiful woman. A beautiful mother."

Nashleigh lifted her purse and groped blindly for a tissue. Her shoulders shook. After some dignified emoting, she covered Giselle's hand with her own and stammered, "I thought you didn't love me. I thought you blamed me for…everything."

Taken aback by her mother's raw words and this unexpected departure from their conversational norms, Giselle asked, "What do you mean?"

"The cleft palate. It happens in the womb. I must have done something—"

"Don't be silly. They don't know why it happens. It can be hereditary, or—"

"Your father used to hit me and kick me when I was pregnant," Nashleigh choked out. "I tried to protect you. You have to believe me."

"Oh, my God. Why didn't you tell me?"

"I didn't want you to think I was poisoning your mind against him."

Stunned, Giselle drained her champagne. For once she and Nashleigh were actually talking. She couldn't understand why she'd never heard any of this before. "I thought it was my fault you and Dad split up."

"God, no. If I hadn't divorced the sonofabitch, I'd have killed him and I'd be at Broward with Grandma Caldwell, and then where would we all be? Not eating morels in this joint, that's for sure."

They fell into silence and Giselle sensed they were equally shaken to find themselves exposing their private wounds all of a sudden. Eventually, she got around to the request she'd been working toward in the first place. "Can I bring Sandy to the wedding?"

"Bring anyone you want." Nashleigh sagged in her chair. "Will she have a partner with her, or will we need to find an escort on the day?"

"She'll bring me. I mean, we'll be escorting each other."

"No, dear." Nashleigh spoke as if Giselle had just suffered a brain-cell die-off. "The best man will be *your* escort. That will leave your friend Sandy *alone*."

This horrifying dilemma was easily solved. Fabio plunked another photo down. "My youngest brother, Romeo. Also handsome."

"Brad Pitt, eat your heart out," Nashleigh crowed.

"He wanted to be a priest," Fabio said. "But there was a problem."

"I'm not surprised." Nashleigh studied the photo closely.

"The low intelligence. So what?" Fabio fretted. "Who cares if a priest does not have this…*mente brillante*? Romeo, he can still have success."

"Yeah, look at our president," Nashleigh offered an inspiring example. "A loser in school, a loser in business. Dumb as dirt. But he made it to the top."

Fabio managed a mournful smile. "Ah, the American dream, no?"

Giselle kept her mouth shut. She had what she wanted. Sandy could come to the wedding. They would be able to escape from the proceedings after a decent interval and explore Tuscany together. What could be more perfect than driving through some of the most romantic countryside in the world with her best friend?

❖

Giselle had started to think Dale would never phone. It had been eight days, not that she was counting.

"You busy right now?" Dale asked.

"No." Giselle muted the television, ashamed to be unemployed and watching *Law & Order* in the afternoon. She was turning into a shut-in.

"There's something I want to show you. I'm illegally parked downstairs."

"That's a contradiction in terms," Giselle scoffed. "You're the police. You can park anywhere."

"That's not the point. Are you coming?"

"Yes." Giselle wondered what was so important that she had to drop everything, or at least the TV remote. She started peeling off her ratty old T-shirt and jeans.

"I'm in a black Crown Victoria." Dale ended the call.

Giselle mumbled, "I'm doing fine. Thanks for asking."

She ran to her room and found a cute navy sundress. After zipping herself into it, she shoved her feet into sandals and took a quick look in the mirror. The dress had a Vargas-girl sensibility that called far too much attention to her breasts. She hitched up the bodice and pulled on a short pink cotton sweater, buttoning it as fast as she could. Satisfied with the modest results, she told herself not to rush as she found her purse and turned things off, but her heart was pumping too fast for her to loll calmly out the door and saunter down to the street.

She reached the bottom step in record time and pushed past a couple of dazed tourists who'd wandered off W. 125th. The man, a solid citizen of pastoral appearance, asked where Rodney King was beaten. Giselle almost didn't bother to reply, but he seemed earnest, so she said politely, "Lake View Terrace. That's in Los Angeles."

The man argued. He appeared to have King confused with some other victim of police brutality. Amadou Diallo. Malcolm Ferguson. Sean Bell. Take your pick.

"Try the 28th Precinct station house," Giselle suggested innocently. "They'll know."

Dale was propped against her car several feet away. Dark glasses, leather jacket, one hand tucked in her belt. Her gun and badge were in plain sight. Giselle let her imagination wander. Dry mouthed, she stared at Dale's belt buckle.

"NYPD," Dale said. "Can I help you folks find something?"

The couple got skittish. The man said, "My wife and I are

members of the ACLU, Ohio."

"And you want to know whose civil rights the enemy has been trampling while we make the streets safe for folks like you?" Dale opened the backseat door and gestured to Giselle. "Get in the car, please, Ms. Truelove."

The visitors both darted apprehensive looks at Giselle.

"Do you need a lawyer, Miss?" the husband asked.

"Come on, Chuck." The wife tugged at him. "I want to go to that soul-food café."

"Smart idea," Dale said.

"If there's a long wait at Sylvia's, try Miss Maude's on Lenox," Giselle suggested as she settled into the car. "Inexpensive and yummy."

Dale gave directions and added, "I recommend the fried chicken."

"Is she under arrest?" Chuck asked, pointing to Giselle.

"In my dreams," Dale said blandly.

The Midwesterners did not know what to make of this. Exchanging puzzled glances, they politely farewelled Dale and scuttled away.

Dale got in the car and started the motor.

Giselle asked, "Why am I in the backseat?"

"Because this is an unmarked NYPD vehicle and I'm still on duty."

"Where are we going?"

"Jersey." Giselle waited for an explanation, but Dale only added, "I can't believe I'm doing this."

They drove sluggishly past brownstones and new stores. The area was crawling with construction crews. Tour groups milled outside various buildings, snapping photographs. Harlem's second Renaissance was hauling them in. W. 125th was starting to look like any other boring shopping precinct in any other city. Old Navy. Ben & Jerry's. Kinkos. Marshall's. Starbucks. Plans for an outlet mall had been shelved after community protests, but the developers weren't going away.

Before her time, Harlem had seemed more like a derelict version of Paris, its once-elegant buildings decayed and burned out, walls plastered with murals. Life had been lived on the streets amidst crack-cocaine turf wars and posses of thugs shaking down grandmas. When Giselle first moved into the neighborhood, the cab driver who transported her from Nashleigh's Upper East Side condo had crossed himself and comforted her with a hug when he saw her new home.

The crime-rate had taken a nosedive in the six years since. Change had its upside.

"What's in Jersey?" she asked the back of Dale's head.

"I have an alibi to check on, then I'm taking you to see the baby."

"Vita?" Giselle was dumbfounded. "I thought you couldn't find out her address."

"Me too, but I called in some favors."

Giselle climbed over the dividing arm and dropped untidily into the front passenger seat, on her knees and back to front. She leaned across and pecked Dale on the cheek.

Dale said, "I knew I shouldn't have taken out that cage."

"Cage?" Giselle turned in the seat, so she was facing forward.

"The partition between front and rear. We usually take them out of unmarked cars so suspects don't realize we're cops."

"That's why there are no handles back there, either? So people can't escape."

"Yes, this is an Interceptor. It's built for police purposes. Ballistic door panels, security glass, and so on."

"Have you ever been shot?" Giselle asked.

"Only once. Just a scratch."

Giselle wondered if Dale was acting tough. "What happened?"

"Put your seat belt on."

They were heading toward the Lincoln Tunnel. Giselle belted up. "Was it a shoot-out?"

"No, an armed robbery in progress. When we asked him to drop his weapon, he opened fire."

"Did you shoot him?"

"My partner did. Winged him. The guy was sentenced to fifteen years."

"He was lucky."

"So was I," Dale said with an edge.

Giselle realized she didn't see Dale, or other cops, as vulnerable. They were the ones with the power and the guns, and the weight of the city behind them if they made a mistake. They were also the ones who rushed to the World Trade Center on 9/11, willing to lose their lives to save strangers. Giselle had always felt confident that if she were in trouble, a cop would help her. But living in Central Harlem had taught her that police benevolence could not be taken for granted by everyone. Plenty of law-abiding citizens had good reason to be wary of law enforcement.

"Are we really going to see Vita?" she asked, still astonished.

"She has another name now," Dale said. "And before you ask, my social-worker buddy didn't give me anything except the address."

"Thank you for doing this."

"It's a one-time-only deal. She's being moved to her permanent family very soon." She glanced at Giselle. "Don't make contact after today. You could cost someone their job."

"I promise."

Giselle watched the double white lines float by and let the roar and whoosh of the tunnel traffic wash over her. Big rigs roared along with their roofs almost scraping the tiled ceiling. One idiot had recently ignored the warning sirens and drove through the tunnel, peeling the top off of his semi.

When she and Dale made it out of the tunnel without incident, she said, "Why didn't you call me?"

"I was waiting until I had some good news."

Giselle felt queasy with disappointment. Dale hadn't been

interested enough to seek her out regardless. She studied the detective's profile. Her chin had a stubborn set, and her mouth was firm and serious. Dark glasses masked her eyes and her thoughts. She drove like it was second nature, both hands on the wheel. In the faint rush of the air-conditioning, her hair wisped back from her forehead. She didn't color it. The tone was a nondescript light brownish blond with a few fine threads of silver emerging at the hairline.

"Why are you single?" Giselle startled herself by asking.

"Been talking with Sandy again?" Dale remarked dryly.

"No, just curious. I don't know if you've noticed but most of the good ones are taken—"

"Which speaks poorly of those of us who are not?" Dale's mouth quirked, creating a dimple in the cheek closest to Giselle. She resisted the urge to place her fingertip in the small hollow.

"Not at all. I assumed you were choosy."

Dale glanced sideways. "Sandy has less flattering words for it."

They both laughed.

Giselle said, "Sandy thinks I should settle down with a genteel art professor who will treat me like a China doll and take me to Europe every summer."

"What do you think?"

"That sounds safe and…dull. Especially the China-doll part."

Giselle noticed a change in Dale's grip on the steering wheel and a sudden tension in her body. The car sped up.

"What went wrong with your last relationship?" Dale asked.

"My ex started sleeping with a man and gave him my job. When I complained, she sacked me."

"That's pretty low. Were you living together?"

"No, thankfully. She hated my apartment."

"She sounds like an idiot."

"And then some. She treated me badly and I put up with her

behavior for far too long. Never again," Giselle articulated the promise she'd made herself. "I deserve better."

"I know the feeling," Dale said.

"We only broke up a couple of weeks ago, but it feels like we were never really together." Giselle mused aloud. "Strange, isn't it? How you can be with someone but it's like you're both strangers?"

Dale nodded slowly. "Yes."

They drove in silence for a while, heading into the green glades of New Jersey.

Eventually, Dale asked, "Do you have plans for this evening, Giselle?"

Giselle's heart picked up speed. "Only if you're inviting me home."

CHAPTER NINE

Y ou have a loft!"
"I think that's overstating it." Dale removed her leather blazer, unfastened her shoulder holster, and placed her 9mm in the top drawer of the writing desk just inside the door. "I opened up two bedrooms to create more space."

Giselle wandered around the living area. "This is fantastic. I love the architecture."

The women Dale brought back to her two-level W. 131st Street condo usually had to hide their astonishment. No one expected a cop's apartment to have a designer feel to it. She'd bought the place when the local dealers were still holding block parties and street crime kept would-be developers at bay. Recently she'd been offered four times what she'd paid.

Giselle continued to enthuse. "It's very modern and simple, yet earthy, too. The found materials add incredible texture. That beaten-copper counter surround with the dark blue bottle glass embedded, what a concept."

Dale hesitated to take all the credit for this unique feature. "Friends of mine have an interior-design business. They built the kitchen. I did most of the other renovations."

"The morning light must be superb," Giselle said. "These tall windows and a rooftop patio. This is to die for."

"I'm not home much during the day to appreciate it." Dale was amused by Giselle's gushy chatter. Apparently she was nervous. "And when I'm not working, I go to Tarrytown to see my mom."

"Of course." Giselle lifted a blown-glass vase from a wall unit and admired it in the fading light before returning it and continuing her tactile tour of the apartment.

Observing her, Dale understood what Sandy was getting at. Giselle was unsophisticated. In her dark blue skirt, flat sandals, and dainty pink cardigan sweater, she looked like a Stepford wife. Dale felt guilty about not calling her until today, but the truth was she'd been putting it off, waiting for her alarming romantic delusions to pass. She'd figured a week would do the trick. It hadn't, and Giselle was now in her apartment, at her invitation, expecting to spend the night—or that's how Dale had read the communication so far.

Giselle was all happy and bubbly and grateful, thrilled to have seen the baby at close quarters. They'd been lucky. The foster mother was wheeling the stroller out for a walk when they arrived, and Giselle had been able to admire the infant at length. She spent most of the trip home talking about how wonderful it was to know that the baby was fine and would grow up in the same kind of dysfunctional, middle-class family most people survived.

"I'm sorry about your mom." Giselle gravitated toward the bookshelves and CD collection on the walls around a seating area. "It must be very stressful."

"It's harder on her than on me."

"How far advanced is the Alzheimer's?"

"She can't remember much and she's been showing signs of dementia lately."

Dale wanted to change the subject. The past week had been a nightmare. Penelope had filed a motion to declare their mother mentally incompetent, proposing herself and Carl as her court-appointed guardians. According to Dale's attorney, this tactic was increasingly employed by yuppies whose parents were inconveniently long-lived and possessed significant estates. Dale would now have to spend her own savings fighting the motion. So much for her overseas holiday.

"How does she manage when you're not there?" Giselle asked. "Is your father—"

"Dad died five years ago." Dale moved the conversation in a more comfortable direction before emotion leaked into her voice. "Can I get you a drink?"

Giselle smiled and swept her dark red hair behind her ears with both hands. "Do you know how to mix a really good martini?"

She barely looked old enough to drink hard liquor. Dale felt about a hundred by comparison. "Sure. I think I can cope."

With a sense of doom, she found a martini glass and set up her cocktail shaker. Here, right in front of her, was the very situation she'd sworn to avoid after leaving Giselle's apartment over a week ago. Firmly under the spell of romance, she'd walked all the way to the two-eight fantasizing about awakening to the smell of fresh coffee and home-baked blueberry muffins, Giselle in her kitchen liked she'd beamed down from a 1950s cookware commercial. To get real, she'd spent the rest of the evening at her desk sorting leads so they'd have a credible suspect for Marvin Small to look at in the next lineup. She needed the distraction.

It had been years since she'd entertained the idea of romance on her own account, but she witnessed the consequences of "love" every day. People literally lost their minds. Rational thinking became the exception, not the rule. Among the ranks of these smitten losers were ordinary, intelligent, respectable people who fell for someone and promptly developed temporary insanity. It could happen.

Dale wasn't the only squad member working unpaid overtime that evening. There were usually a few extras at the station house for the night shift, guys whose wives had kicked them out, or who'd had a rough day and needed to wind down. It was a safe bet that anyone holed up at their desk unnecessarily after midnight had a sob story to tell, usually love-related. Afraid to ask, Dale stayed in her seat with her head down, doing her best to absorb the business-as-usual din around her, so she could be reminded of who she was. There was something comforting about listening to squad members picking up the phone, eating pizza, griping about nuisance calls, and taking turns sleeping in interview rooms.

Like every other precinct, the two-eight had its share of regulars rousted from their street corners when there was nothing better to do. The usual suspects were there that evening, yelling requests from the holding tank and singing "Mona Lisa" and other hit tunes of days gone by. These habitual offenders treated lockup as a social opportunity, the highlight of their week. Dale had found that, treated decently, street people could be a valuable resource, keeping detectives in touch with gossip and anything unusual that went down. She'd spent some time with a couple of homeless guys that night, just in case there was talk about the bodega killing. Marvin Small could not be the only witness, but for some reason the others were intimidated.

As usual, her questions met with blank stares and exaggerated shrugs. Dale was fine with that. In the holding tank, no one could afford to look like a snitch. After they were back on the streets, she would follow up discreetly.

So far, her strategy hadn't produced any solid new leads, but the case was only four weeks old. Eventually, when the heat was off, a pissed-off ex-girlfriend would talk, or the shooter would run off at the mouth, thinking it was safe to brag. Homicide investigation was about patience and a long memory, not just about the crime scene.

Feeling more centered after her reassuring digression into work, she measured out the correct balance of gin and dry vermouth, asking, "Stirred or shaken? Dusky or dirty?"

"You choose." Giselle gave one of her small, uneven smiles, and it occurred to Dale that she probably thought her scarred lip would be too obvious if she didn't guard her expressions.

She added a dash of brine, stirred the martini, and strained it over a couple of olives. For herself, she poured Sambuca over ice, a drink she wasn't crazy about and probably wouldn't finish, a blessing since she didn't need her mind softened by alcohol when all she had to do was look at her guest.

Giselle had just unbuttoned the nice-girl sweater and draped it over the back of the sofa. She wasn't wearing a skirt, as Dale had thought, but a sexy dress that strained around her flawless breasts. Willing herself not to think about handling them, Dale carried the drinks to the coffee table near the front windows before hastening back to the kitchen to find some snack food.

Giselle flipped diligently through the music options. "Disco is alive and well in the Porter home, I see."

Dale didn't explain that she had an ex to thank for the Bee Gees and Abba selections.

Giselle put on one of the jazz mixes burned from her favorite playlists. John Coltrane. Billie Holliday. Louis Armstrong. Humming along, she inspected the narrow floor-to-ceiling bookcases behind the sofa, observing, "Don't you get depressed reading all these gruesome books?"

Dale didn't answer right away. Being a homicide detective could be depressing; certainly she had a heightened sense of her own mortality and no illusions about the human condition. But she didn't want to get into a heavy conversation. "I'm doing school part-time so I can finish my master's degree." At Giselle's startled blink, she added, "Some of the more specialized investigative techniques interest me."

"I guess DNA evidence has changed everything for detectives."

"To some extent," Dale conceded. "We can rule out suspects more quickly now. That's a big help. But most times, we don't have much physical evidence to work with, especially not the kind that holds up in a trial. The burden of proof is higher than it used to be."

"Because of CSI?"

Dale nodded. "Juries have unrealistic expectations. They're

waiting for experts to wheel out a truckload of hard scientific evidence, and they think you're sloppy if you haven't found any. Then, if you do find it, they focus on bullshit like police tampering and sample contamination, like the verdict rests on a scrap of DNA, which it seldom does." She paused, hearing her own frustration. Giselle appeared interested in this lecture on building a case, but perhaps she was just being diplomatic. Dale concluded, "In real life, investigating crimes and getting convictions is a lot less glamorous than you see on TV."

"And I notice you don't wear the really tight pants and plunging necklines, either." A small twist altered Giselle's mouth, making Dale want to kiss her.

"Yeah, my partner thinks *CSI Miami* should be mandatory viewing for female officers so we get with the program."

"So, how do you convict people without the scientific evidence?"

"It's all about the confession," Dale said. "That's why they're so important. And the strange thing is, most of the time people give it up, and you don't have to beat a statement out of them. Physical coercion is pointless."

Giselle gave her a look that was almost tender. "You don't need to explain that to me. I would never take you for a bent cop."

Dale was silent for a moment, arranging crackers on the plate she'd piled with cheese and grapes. She hadn't realized she was defending herself automatically. She gave a rueful smile. "You got me."

"For what it's worth, I admire the job you do," Giselle said sincerely. "I wish a few of your colleagues didn't earn the rest of you a bad name, but that's life." Sitting neatly in one corner of the sofa, she'd just made herself comfortable when Dale's cat, Colonel Kurtz, leapt up and pudged his way to the deep leather cushion next to her.

"Be careful," Dale warned, carrying a plate of cheese and fruit over. "He seems friendly but he can turn."

"Sounds like my ex."

Dale set the plate down with some napkins and forks. "Just wait. Kurtz is manipulative, too. He's not allowed cheese, but he'll be all over you, begging for it, because he thinks you don't know the rules."

Sure enough, the hefty tabby started purring and rolling. He regarded the cheese then stared up at Giselle like she was a goddess.

"Kurtz," she echoed pensively. *Apocalypse Now*?

"It seemed fitting." Dale handed the martini to her and settled at the other end of the sofa. "He's just a little obsessive."

"I think it's a good sign when a cat decides to adore you. They're picky and they always know a fake when they see one."

"I guess that explains why he peed in one of my ex's shoes. It's the only time he ever messed."

Laughing, they tapped glasses and Giselle sipped her drink. "It's perfect. Thank you."

Dale wondered how much longer they would have to sustain the impersonal chitchat while they covertly sized each other up. Giselle's long, silky eyelashes veiled her scrutiny, but Dale knew when she was being watched. "I'm not sure how hungry you are, but I have a chicken-and-basil salad, or we could go out, if you prefer."

Giselle shook her head. "The salad sounds good."

The setting sun aimed bright gold shafts into the room, forcing her to shield her eyes. Her hair glowed ember-red in the intense light, making her skin seem translucently pale. For the first time, Dale noticed a fine dusting of freckles across her nose and elegant cheekbones. She could also see the twist of her scar, like a thread of white silk trapped beneath the surface of her flesh.

Her mouth was beautiful regardless, the full top lip arched deliciously above the sensuous bottom. She took another sip of martini and licked the residue away. Mesmerized, Dale caught her breath and tried to get ahold of herself. She rose and adjusted the blinds. Something was wrong. In the car, despite her intentions to the contrary, she had decided to sleep with Giselle. Her rationale was straightforward: they were physically attracted. They would have sex, date for a few weeks, and then part when they were ready. In theory, it sounded fine. Dale only wished she didn't lapse into strange sentimentality in Giselle's presence. The emotions made her uneasy because she had so little control over them. The woman was just sitting on her sofa, drinking her martini, and patting Colonel Kurtz. She was not lounging provocatively, breasts jutting, legs parted, eyes half-closed, begging Dale to fuck her.

The thought made Dale weak and also presented her with a blinding flash of the obvious: the reason she had mixed feelings about sleeping with Giselle was that her thinking was sexist. She'd been on the force too long, absorbing the value judgments of the mostly male detectives she worked with. No matter how enlightened they thought they were, most clung to the old dichotomy. There were wives, mothers, daughters, sisters, and "decent" girls. And there were sluts, whores, offenders, and girlfriends of offenders.

Dale didn't know Giselle beyond first impressions, yet she had already placed her in the "nice-girls-who-get-married" category, as opposed to "bad girls who like sex," the pool from which Dale usually chose her companions. As a consequence, she felt protective and responsible, and weirdly guilty for wanting to take off Giselle's clothes and make love to her. In the back of her mind lurked the uneasy belief that if she slept with Giselle she was somehow agreeing to a relationship, not just a few hot dates. While nothing was wrong with relationships, Dale didn't have the energy to work on one, and the last thing she wanted was to hurt a sweet woman like Giselle, who deserved more than she could offer.

Giselle directed a quizzical stare at her. "Is something wrong?"

Dale could not come up with the appropriate reply. "I'll fix that chicken salad."

"No, wait. I have a better idea."

Reluctantly, Dale returned to her corner of the sofa. She was bothered by her own navel-gazing, acutely aware that one key element was missing from her deliberations: what did Giselle want?

Lifting Colonel Kurtz, Giselle slid across the leather cushions so her thigh was brushing Dale's. She placed the tabby on the warm impression she'd just left. Remarkably, he curled up without protests.

In a serious tone, she said, "Stop analyzing everything. Who knows what tomorrow will bring? This is now." She lifted Dale's hand to her lips and placed a kiss in the palm. "Let's skip dinner and go to bed."

Dale almost fell off the sofa. She had expected they would slowly work their way around to this option, and she had expected to do the propositioning herself. Wanting to give them both a way out, she mumbled, "Are you sure?"

Giselle transported Dale's hand beneath her skirt and cupped it to her panties. "What do you think?"

Dale groaned a soft, "Oh, God."

Giselle felt Dale's fingers curl against the thin, lacy barrier. She watched Dale's tongue intrude briefly on her lips, moistening them. She knew what was coming and sidestepped the impending kiss by lowering her head in a show of embarrassment. Reaching around, she unzipped her dress, and slid it from her shoulders. Dale's hot gaze immediately fell to her breasts. Her breathing grew unsteady. She withdrew her hand from between Giselle's legs and stood, drawing Giselle with her.

The sundress dropped to the floor, and Giselle stepped out of it. Before she could pick up the garment, Dale swept her into her arms and strode through the apartment as if there was nothing remotely unusual in carrying a woman this way.

The bedroom they entered was stark but comfortable, and unmistakably Dale's. She set Giselle on the large, neatly made bed. Without looking away from her once, she folded the bedding back, pausing only to give Giselle time to raise her hips so the covers could slide away beneath her.

Her gray eyes darkening with promise, she leaned over Giselle, one hand flat on the pillow by her right shoulder. "You're beautiful," she said huskily.

She ran a fingertip delicately back and forth over Giselle's lips, teasing them apart. Giselle slid her tongue around Dale's finger and took it briefly into her mouth, sucking, holding her stare, watching her pupils enlarge.

She reached down to remove her panties but Dale said, "No. Not yet."

Her voice was hoarse with desire. Giselle knew what she wanted as plainly as if she had told her, as if they shared an aura of complete understanding. Bashful at the thought, she covered her breasts with one arm and lowered her gaze. A little apprehensively, she said, "I haven't slept with a woman for quite a while. Bobbi and I were kind of…over it."

"Over it," Dale repeated as if the words were in another language. Frowning, she got to her feet and removed her shirt.

She wore a white sports-style midriff bra over breasts that were strictly minimalist, the nipples light brown. Tan lines created a paler expanse of skin in the shape of a tank T-shirt, and she wore no chains. Unfastening her belt, she continued to undress without a hint of self-consciousness. She had to know she had a great body.

When she was down to her plain black briefs, she stretched out a hand to Giselle. "Let's shower."

She led the way to a large bathroom adjoining her bedroom. It was tiled in a rich mix of colors that contrasted surprisingly with the plain cream tones of her bedroom. Travertine floor, mosaic walls and shower, and a sunken tub below a skylight; the combination spoke of a room in which the owner liked to relax, not just wash. The shower easily accommodated two people and even had a recess that could double as a seat or shelf.

Dale turned on the water and drew Giselle into her arms. They held each other for a long time, then Dale's hands moved down past the small of Giselle's back collecting the panties and sliding them off. Giselle watched Dale do the same and could not remember the last time she'd stood in a room naked with a woman she wanted so badly. The thought made her sad.

"Giselle?" Dale adjusted the temperature and held the shower door for her.

The water was pleasantly hot, but not energy-draining.

Giselle reached for the soap, but Dale said, "Let me."

She came closer, letting their bodies brush and slide as she soaped and caressed. She lingered over Giselle's breasts and butt. Her hands were firm and never quite abandoned their mission to clean. She worked on herself at the same time, so that they were both slippery. Giselle joined the exploration, kneading and squeezing and swapping loofah for soap and sponge. Cocooned together in the warm storm of the water, they didn't speak a word, lost in a sensual dialogue that brought them closer and closer until, quite abruptly, the rules changed.

Dale's mouth clamped on her nipple and her knee was between Giselle's legs. Each hand claimed a breast. Giselle felt weak. She sagged back against the tiled shelf, aware that she was dripping slick, silken fluids the warm water could not disperse.

Dale killed the shower. They stumbled out. She wrapped Giselle in a large white towel and patted herself down with another. Giselle's mind was clouded. Her lips were dry. She kept licking them but it made no difference. All the moisture in her body seemed to have settled south, drenching her inner thighs. She was afraid to look at Dale, knowing what was to come. Dale was bigger and stronger than her, sinewy and solidly muscled, very different from the slightly built lovers Giselle usually chose.

Nerves made Giselle's stomach flutter. Everything seemed to be moving too fast. Her body felt overly sensitive. Her nipples hurt so much the soft pile of the towel rasped unkindly. She ached at her core, needing relief, nearly whimpering at the grinding pressure inside. Dale's hand closed over the front of the towel, but Giselle could not let go. She wished she'd finished her martini.

With a knowing smile, Dale took Giselle's face between her hands and stared into her eyes. "It's okay if you want to change your mind. There's always the chicken salad."

Feeling foolish, Giselle relinquished the towel. Her hands shook. Goose bumps tightened her skin. She gazed past Dale at their image in the bathroom mirror, her pale self against the darker, broader frame of her companion. The sight made her crave Dale's touch with such intensity she shivered.

"You're chilled." Dale's hand pressed warmly between her shoulders. "Come to bed."

A few seconds later, they were in each other's arms between cool, soft linen, their faces just inches apart. To Giselle's surprise, Dale was shaking. She glimpsed a fleeting disquiet in her eyes, but before she could ask what was wrong, Dale's mouth was on hers. Without ceremony, she stole the kiss Giselle had withheld. She tasted of aniseed. Her tongue transferred the flavor, probing deeply, demanding acceptance. Giselle kissed her hungrily in return, making promises of her own. They barely paused for breath. Dale dragged her tongue along the inside of Giselle's upper lip, tenderly, delicately sucking. At the same time, she parted Giselle's legs, jerking a low, animal sound from the back of her throat.

Giselle arched her back so she could meet the tantalizing brush of Dale's fingertips. Her breath came in short, sharp bursts. She begged, "Yes."

"Yes, what?" Dale had not stopped kissing her.

"Anything." Giselle gasped against her lips. "Anything you want."

Dale regarded her with eyes like sin. "Right now I want to fuck your mouth, but that can wait."

Shock only made her arousal more excruciating. Disconcerted by a vivid flash of herself sucking Dale and making her come, Giselle moaned and linked her hands behind Dale's neck. She could feel Dale's nipples against her chest. They were just as stiff as her own. Dale's mouth left hers and she was pinned down hard, flat on her back. Volition fled her, and her hands fell on either side of her head, in surrender.

Instead of going down on her, like lovers always did, Dale spread her open. Eyes glinting, she murmured, "You're very wet. Is this what I do for you?"

Giselle's nerves screamed with anticipation. "I'm going to come any moment. I can't bear it."

"Good." Dale dipped her fingers, sliding past Giselle's clit just firmly enough to make her writhe with need.

Giselle threw her head back, losing herself in the gentle, prolonged strokes, the teasing twists, and the exquisite torture of Dale's fingers working back and forth. She couldn't belief how aroused she was. It was never like this. She never had this helpless compulsion to come quickly and violently. She could feel the orgasm hammering at her center. A clamoring need spread through her whole body, making her breasts swell and her skin burn.

She lifted her hips, and Dale responded by rocking her knuckle against her clit, crushing the soaking flesh splayed on either side. The sense of a hard, rounded ball of flesh at her opening made Giselle spill more profusely. She needed Dale inside her. The thick, panting plea she heard could not be her own.

Dale's eyes glowed with fierce hunger. "I want you coming all over me." She slid a small way in. "Oh, God."

Giselle sensed her control and squirmed with impatience, desperate for more. Dale pushed slowly, easing back when she struck resistance and gradually sliding deeper. Giselle lifted one hand and let it rest against Dale's face. At the same time, she moved her pelvis forcefully to meet Dale's next stroke, taking her rapidly inside. A sharp cry was drawn from her at the mixture of pain and pleasure, and Dale froze for a moment, comprehension cramping her features.

Leaving her hand where it was, she slid her free arm beneath Giselle and cradled her close, kissing her deeply. Her skin was damp and hot. They were both panting and sweating.

"Don't stop," Giselle whispered.

For a split second she felt empty, then Dale opened her a little more. "You want me?"

"Yes."

"Like this."

"Yes."

"Oh, fuck." Dale released Giselle from the tight embrace. Her weight shifted and she was between Giselle's legs, pushing her knees wide apart. Her strokes changed. She plunged in faster and harder, her thumb bearing down on Giselle's clit.

Giselle seized her shoulders, digging her nails into the muscles working below the smooth skin. Deep within, she felt a primal pulse gathering strength, sucking the energy from the rest of her body. She no longer had the strength to hold Dale or even to speak. The molten pressure at her core was so intense, she could only give in to it, crying out as she lost all control. A profound spasm shook her body, radiating out in a series of mini-shocks like nothing she had ever known.

Mingling with her own cries, she heard Dale's and realized her own startling release was shared. They clung together, raggedly breathing, occasionally trading shattered kisses. When Dale's weight grew heavy, Giselle reluctantly placed a hand against her chest and Dale propped herself up. Carefully, by degrees, she withdrew from Giselle, and rolled onto her side.

They stared at each other for a long time.

"I don't know what to say." Dale seemed shell-shocked. She examined the hand she'd just liberated from Giselle's body.

Giselle could still feel the impression of her fingers. "Are words necessary?"

"No." Dale kissed her, a delicate brush of the lips.

They curled into each other, completely entwined. Giselle felt sore, but in a good way. She closed her eyes and inhaled Dale's scent, salty and musky. They both smelled of sex. Already she wanted to make love again, this time to give Dale what she craved. Drifting, she smiled, blissfully happy.

CHAPTER TEN

Dale washed sexual residue from her hands and inspected a mottled bite mark on her shoulder, one of several her shirt would need to hide when she dressed for work. She hovered in front of the bathroom mirror, puzzling over the stroke of luck—or not—that made her attractive to women. Some of her short-term girlfriends had theories about why they were drawn to her and liked to expound on these by way of accounting for the time they'd wasted trying to have a relationship with her. The X-factor. Pheromones. Body language. Androgyny. Dominance. Butch attitude. Good hands. Fond of animals. Dale had also encountered women who *loved* the idea that she was a cop. These groupies were all about the fantasy and wanted the usual role-playing. After spending most of her working day trying to arrest people in real time, Dale found the idea of slapping handcuffs on a lover routine, to say the least. So those liaisons didn't last long.

She knew, from the second glances she received, that she wasn't bad looking. Being tall, confident, and in shape helped. She also dressed well and had a decent hairdresser, even if he constantly bemoaned her boring style and her failure to invest in highlights. He didn't understand the desire to blend in, but Dale had found out, early in her career, that if she wanted to be taken seriously on the job, looking like she spent half her life fixing her hair was unhelpful.

She turned off the faucets, dried her hands, and took a last look in the mirror. Nothing in her facial features stood out. She'd inherited her father's long nose and determined jaw. Every time she looked in a mirror, his candid gray eyes stared back at her. She liked that.

Flicking off the light, she hovered in the bathroom doorway, waiting for her eyes to adjust to the darkness. She could just make out Giselle's shape on the bed. Like the baby in her painting, she slept curled up on her side. A few hours after their last lovemaking, Dale had attempted to spoon with her, but Giselle had shuffled away. Dale wasn't offended. She liked to sleep alone, too. Usually, she had a hard time with companions who needed to be all over her.

Mystified by her rare urge to cuddle, she padded across the wood floor and slid into bed. Giselle didn't stir, and Dale almost laughed at her own disappointment. Briefly she considered waking the sleeping woman so they could make love again. But she'd already given in to the same powerful urge twice and would feel bad about dragging Giselle from a deep sleep a third time. Suppressing her desires, she rolled away from temptation and hunched restlessly on the edge of the bed.

Giselle's body needed some recovery time, she reasoned to further douse her desires. What kind of oaf would insist on having her way when sex was becoming uncomfortable? Dale was just perverted enough to allow herself a smile. She liked that she was the oaf responsible for Giselle's tender state.

It hadn't crossed her mind, when they were first making love, that a woman who'd been in several relationships would still have a partially intact hymen. She felt vaguely disgusted that she could even think about Giselle in such clinical terms, but such was the homicide detective's mindset. At the time, she'd been so shocked to meet the unexpected barrier that she'd almost called a halt to the proceedings. But Giselle had seemed very determined, and who was Dale to say no to a lovely, willing woman? She'd duly rationalized that Giselle was just one of the unlucky few with an anatomical quirk that made certain activities difficult. No doubt she knew her own limitations.

Much later, after they'd made love again and Giselle had demonstrated advanced oral skills, Dale had asked a few personal questions. The answers shocked her. Giselle had somehow spent most of her history with partners who were perfectly happy to go without sex for months at a time. On the rare occasions they did get down to it, they were neither adventurous nor enthusiastic. Giselle blamed herself for their lack of interest and had presented Dale with a warped theory about women being turned off after kissing her.

Based on the evidence, Dale suspected Giselle had been playing out some kind of pattern, dating unresponsive women so she wouldn't have to deal with her own unease about the lip disfigurement. Her most recent girlfriend had done her a favor by making her angry. At least now she might try something new.

Frowning, Dale thought about her own patterns. She dated women who were hot to have sex with her and she never paid much attention to potential compatibility in any other sphere. Once the sexual chemistry fizzled, there was no reason to keep on dating, so she moved on. Every so often, when she sank into angst about her single state, she tried the committed-relationship route. And failed.

The loss of her few meaningful relationships bothered her intensely. She chose women she thought she could love and respect, and she developed bonds. She tried hard to create balance between her work and personal lives. But in each of the three relationships that really mattered to her over the years, something had gone badly wrong.

Her first serious partner had been incredibly insecure about Dale's job and, in the end, had made her choose. After that split, Dale settled down with a woman who had children. That was a disaster. She always felt like an outsider, but she did her best to provide a good home and be a supportive co-parent. When her partner decided to go back to hubby, Dale felt used and betrayed. It took a long time to move beyond that curveball.

Her third attempt at the real thing had been doomed from the start. Dale had done what many cops do and "married" someone on the force, imagining a partner who would understand the stresses and demands of the job and not expect the impossible. The relationship had lasted less than a year, ending in bitterness and recriminations. Her partner had seen Dale as competition and was infuriated when she was promoted to detective. In her anger, she embarked on a secret vendetta to undermine Dale at work, including filing an anonymous complaint with Internal Affairs.

After that fiasco Dale had decided that she was better off single. Not faux single: actively looking but pretending to love the "freedom." Or unhappily single: sorry for herself and jealous of everyone in a relationship. Or default single: dumped and hanging out for the next heartbreak. Or insecure single: dateless but pretending to be picky. No, she was getting all the goodies without the hassle. She was happy, guilt-free, and determined to stay that way. As far as she was concerned, she could not be single enough.

She hadn't suffered a moment of self-doubt about her state for several years. Being single suited her in every way. Life was short, and Dale didn't plan to spend hers justifying herself to a partner who couldn't accept her for who she was. It blew her away that women could claim undying love and then try to turn her into someone else.

Sandy was always telling her to find a woman who had no agenda other than the relationship. She thought Dale had been suckered by partners who wanted to use her, and when she didn't play her role, the relationships were history. At one time, Dale had wondered if she and Sandy could get together. They hit it off the moment they met, and they'd talked about the possibility. But somehow they'd never taken the next step, and the stronger their friendship grew, the less Dale wanted to risk losing it. They had agreed some time ago that they would never have a fling because people got weird afterwards. As for anything serious, there was no way.

Dale cringed at the thought of telling her friend about last night. Recently, Sandy had hatched a plan to introduce Giselle to a closeted bank vice-president with an interest in art and a penchant for sweet little femmes. She thought they'd be a perfect match and had been planning the "chance encounter" for weeks. Dale wasn't sure of the details, but all of a sudden she wanted to know.

She shifted across the bed and enfolded Giselle from behind. Trailing feather-soft kisses over her nape, she murmured, "I can't sleep with you lying here next to me. I want you in the worst way."

It was only 4:30 a.m. If they made love now, she could still catch some sleep before she had to go to work.

❖

"Let me help you with that." Sandy lifted a tangle of yellow emergency tape away from a woman whose cling wrap had been pulled loose from her hair, which was plastered with straightener. They both spent some time re-wrapping her head.

While they were preoccupied, a tall chestnut horse clopped by with a cop in the saddle, a sight unseen in the neighborhood until recently. Giselle glanced around and spotted at least four uniformed officers and a patrol car. She was also aware of several Crown Victorias crawling along near the curb. Unmarked cars. Heavy policing had become the norm on Lenox Avenue now that white people were walking up from Central Park to buy their Starbucks in the newly opened Harlem store.

She and Sandy continued past Sylvia's familiar blue awning. The restaurant had been a favorite of theirs before it became a tour-bus destination. Since then, the food quality had declined, the prices were hiked, and the noise level was unbearable. Giselle didn't mind waiting an hour for collard greens and candied yams if they were sensational. But while she twiddled her thumbs, she didn't want to hear the Lord praised every two minutes by a big-bosomed gospel singer who roved the tables asking tourists where they were from.

Once a month, she and Sandy indulged themselves in a soul-food experience. Today, they were eating at the Lenox Lounge. A favorite of Giselle's, the club had started opening for lunch recently. 9/11 had seen a downturn in visitors and the demise of numerous hole-in-the-wall soul-food cafes around the area. Venues opened and closed all the time, leaving the venerable bastions to handle the ebb and flow. Giselle paused in the wide boulevard, waiting for another herd of tourists to finish snapping photos of the front entrance. Most then drifted down a block to W. 123rd where a row of Italianate brownstones had been restored, reminding passersby of Harlem's former splendor.

Sandy cut a path through the out-of-towners and waved impatiently from the paneled door of the Lounge. Giselle scuttled to join her. The front bar was packed with Columbia students, and both jukebox and TV were turned up loud. The restaurant was quieter and only half full. They found a table at a discreet distance from other diners, and Sandy, always on a timetable, immediately ordered her usual mac and cheese. Giselle ordered fried whiting without looking the menu. She'd only taken a few sips of water when Sandy's gaze locked on a woman several tables away.

"You have to be kidding me. Francesca Larson?" She stood up and asked Giselle to excuse her.

Apparently they were old friends, if the kissing on both cheeks was any indication. Francesca belonged in the Zebra Room. She wore a three-piece suit that quietly intimated custom tailoring. In a subtle charcoal pinstripe, it hugged a lithe physique. Her hair was black and smoothly cut in a style that looked like 1920s Berlin. The choice was no accident of silly hairdressing, but the ideal frame for a face so perfect Giselle thought her mouth had probably fallen open in wonder.

Sandy said something and her stunning friend cast a look across the restaurant. Giselle had the impression of dark, disturbing eyes above dramatic cheekbones. Like a klutz, she stumbled to her feet as Sandy herded the sublime stranger over.

After performing the introductions, Sandy asked, "Would you mind if Francesca joined us?"

"No. Not at all." Giselle winced as she sat down. She was so sore *she* needed one of those rubber donut cushions Sandy talked about. Her nipples, also painful, tightened at the thought of her night with Dale, and she caught her breath. On some level, she was relieved that they were no longer in private. She'd been about to spill the whole story, but it could wait. She would love not to have to deal with the lecture and eye-rolling.

"Sandy mentioned you paint," Francesca said in a smooth, cultured voice.

"It's just a hobby."

"I helped my father build his art collection." Francesca's smile was warm but contained. "I suppose that could be considered a hobby also."

"I hope you don't mind, Giselle," Sandy interjected. "I showed Francesca some photographs of your paintings."

Giselle's cheeks flamed. The very idea of a serious art collector finding fault in her amateur efforts made her want to shrink under the table.

"Now you're embarrassed." Francesca placed a cool hand fleetingly on Giselle's. "Please don't be. Contemporary portraiture is an abiding passion of mine. Where did you study?"

"I've taken a few evening classes, but basically I've taught myself."

"Remarkable. I would not have guessed that." Francesca offered an indulgent smile. "In fact, my first impression was RISD."

Giselle had to think for a moment about what she'd said. It sounded like "rizdee." Rhode Island School of Design.

"It's impossible to judge from a photograph, naturally," Francesca waxed on. "But your work has a humble intimacy I find most appealing. Your use of light is quite striking, almost surreal. The manner in which you bring such prominence to the face. The floating sensibility you conveyed in your portrait of the janitor…" With a self-effacing shrug, she said, "As you can tell, I'm quite the enthusiast. I would very much like to view your originals."

"You would?"

"Where do you have your studio?"

"I paint at home, in my apartment." Giselle slowed her speech, taking care not to let her tongue move too freely. She didn't want to sound like a lisping child to this sophisticate. "I'd be happy to show you what I'm working on."

"I'm free this afternoon," Francesca said.

Sandy stood abruptly. "I'm being paged. Please excuse me."

"Certainly." Francesca rose with an old-fashioned courtesy that was plainly second nature.

Her elegance took Giselle's breath away. How many women would have the lean-hipped frame to get away with wearing a suit like hers? Not to mention the panache. The cut was very masculine. The shoulder width provided almost the only clue that the jacket was made for a woman. Curious, Giselle glanced down at Francesca's hands, attempting to guess her age. Forty-five, she decided, but with the remarkable bone structure, her face seemed ageless. She would make a fascinating subject.

"And you, Giselle?" Francesca pronounced her name as the French did. "Do you have a little time to spare today?"

"Yes." Giselle wished she'd cleaned house. She'd only managed to tidy up quickly before getting back from Dale's place and leaving for lunch.

Dale. Her pulse started to climb, and she was profoundly

aware of her wet panties and swollen flesh. She wanted another kiss. She still couldn't believe how wonderful their kissing had been. How she forgot that she'd ever felt ugly. Dale was not in relation to what was wrong, only what was right.

She had left a note for Giselle that morning. It read:

Hey, beautiful.

Stay in bed all day, if you want. I'll phone later. Did I tell you how sexy you are? You wrecked my concentration for the day. I hope you're satisfied. Really, really satisfied.

Dale

Giselle's nipples distracted her, gouging at the flimsy fabric of her top. She wished she'd worn a light sweater and jeans, but she and Sandy had a deal. She wore clothes from the scant premium end of her wardrobe when they went out, so that Sandy wouldn't feel overdressed. Self-consciously she glanced down. It was all she could do not to lay her hands over her breasts. Her nipples stuck out like fingertips, prodding the thin, dove-gray rayon of her shirt. The top was loose and short, just covering the waistband of her silk chiffon skirt.

Francesca wasn't blind. Her eyes lifted from Giselle's chest. Not a ripple disturbed the serenity of her face. "Are you interested in self-portraiture?"

"I've never thought about it."

"I purchased a nude study recently," she said in a reflective tone. "It's not a fine work but the silent tension is fascinating. When I made inquiries I discovered it was a self-portrait."

Sandy was back. She'd picked up her mac and cheese to go. "I'm sorry to run out on you both." She touched Francesca's arm. "I've been meaning to call. You know how that goes."

Francesca was back on her feet and performed the European

cheek-kissing ritual with Sandy once more. Velvet-voiced, she said, "It was good to see you again."

Their food was on the table. After slipping into her seat, Francesca tackled the only menu item that wouldn't lethally clog her arteries—black-eyed peas. Giselle had the impression soul food wasn't her preferred fare. Why would she journey uptown to a place like this when she clearly belonged at The Modern?

"How did you meet Sandy?" Giselle asked.

"We met at a fundraiser several years ago. She gave me some good advice concerning a delicate matter and we kept in touch."

Giselle poked at her whiting. It looked good but she wasn't hungry. Her stomach churned with a mixture of anticipation and desire. The hours could not go by fast enough. Dale would call soon. They would see each other tonight. She wasn't sure how much sex she could handle, since she'd almost given herself an orgasm crossing her legs under the table. But she could lavish her attentions on Dale. Somehow her taste and smell still clung to the lining of Giselle's mouth and nose, insistently present even after she'd cleaned her teeth. She smiled at the thought and knew she'd colored again.

"What are you thinking?" Francesca's gaze was very direct.

"I'm excited." Giselle tried to stay close to the truth.

"I can see that."

"I never show anyone my work."

"Then I'm honored." Francesca wet her chiseled lips almost imperceptibly and waved for the check.

CHAPTER ELEVEN

N ow that your guest has departed, I need you to be my nurse for a couple of hours," Dr. Redman said. This was his second phone call. Francesca had still been poring over Giselle's paintings when he made the first.

"How can I be your nurse?" Giselle protested. "I don't know the difference between a scalpel and a retractor."

"You know the names. That's something." He added, "I'll pay you."

"Will it take long?" Giselle checked the time. Three thirty. Maybe her mission would be accomplished before Dale showed up.

"An hour," Dr. Redman said. "I know I don't need to mention my role in baby Vita's critical first forty-eight hours."

Giselle gasped in outrage. Emotional blackmail was not Dr. Redman's style. "Are you drunk?"

"Don't be absurd." He chuckled. "Of course I'm drunk."

"Well, that's a problem." Giselle saw herself being led away in handcuffs, the fake nurse of a drunk doctor practicing without a license.

He said, "You don't know the half of it."

"Alright, you win. What do I need to wear?"

"It won't matter. You'll be in scrubs."

"I'm not cutting into a person's body," she insisted. "Not even for two hundred dollars worth of freshly squeezed breast milk."

She dropped the receiver, then immediately grabbed it again and called Dale. Predictably, she reached voice mail. She left a message. "I'm downstairs at Dr. Redman's. You can reach me on my cell phone." She wanted to say something personal, but hesitated in case she came across as clingy. Given Dale's track record, a sexy comment was probably her best option. Hoping for sultry, she said, "I've been wet all day, thinking about you."

On that note, she ended the call and hurried down to bang on Dr. Redman's door.

He all but yanked her into his living room. Thrusting a plastic bag full of green clothing at her, he said, "Put these on to protect your clean outfit."

"Is the patient here?"

"Yes." He could hardly stand. He smelled of cheap scotch, not the usual fine single malt. His eyes were unfocused.

Giselle started pulling the scrubs on over her dress. "You can't operate. You're a mess. I know they're mostly criminals, but they trust you and you're taking their money."

His laughter was caustic, the gentlemanly facade in pieces. "Come into the surgical suite when you're ready."

Giselle finished putting on her nurse disguise and went into the kitchen. She made coffee and wrapped an icepack in a cloth, the usual remedies when she found her neighbor rolling drunk. Leaving both on the counter, she knocked and entered the spare room, expecting to see a Blood from East Harlem sprawled on the operating table and his fifteen-year-old girlfriend parked in a corner sniffing into a red bandanna.

Instead, Dr. Redman lay there. On a medical cart next to him, a series of syringes lay in a row. He had an IV catheter in his arm.

"What's going on?" Giselle asked.

"I intended to take care of this myself, but I confess, I have some concerns about becoming vegetative instead."

Giselle stared down at the needles as sick suspicion caught

hold of her. She reached for words but her mouth was dry with horror.

"We're not going to do this all at once," he said. "First, the matter of your payment. The cash box on the mantel. You'll find about two thousand dollars in cash there. That's for you to have and use as you please. Go get a pretty dress."

"Dr. Redman, I can see where this is headed, and—"

"I know, my dear Giselle. It's morally repugnant to you. That's why I shall carry out every function myself. All I ask—"

"No," Giselle cried. "You think I'm going to watch you take your own life? You think I'll go help myself to your cash afterward and buy new clothes?"

He ignored her outburst and continued his calm farewell speech. "With the cash, you'll also find the key to a safe-deposit box at the Apple Bank. You'll see what to do with the contents. I've left instructions."

Giselle shook her head. "I refuse. I won't allow this. I'm going to call the police."

"So they can talk me down from the roof, to the applause of the mob who will, the very next day, spit as I walk by?"

"Listen to yourself. You're too drunk to make a big decision like this one. If you jumped off our roof you'd probably only break your legs."

"I used an analogy."

Giselle sat down on the chair next to the operating table. "Why are you doing this? Why today?"

"What will tomorrow change?" What light there was drained out of his face, leaving his sorrow naked. "The truth is that no matter what happens, whether you stay or leave, I've made my date with eternity and I shall keep it."

"I need to understand." Giselle rested her head on the clean white cotton next to his. She laid an arm across his chest. "Close your eyes. Pretend it's nighttime. Late in the quiet hours. Just talk to the darkness, like you're all alone."

His chest heaved like something monstrous rose within. His voice shook. "Until today I could always hope. When there's no body, that's what happens, you see. You don't want to believe your child is gone. You're in a limbo, trapped between worlds. All you can do is wait. Everything is about marking time until the waiting ends. And today it did."

"Miranda?" Giselle whispered.

"They found her body."

Tears drowned Giselle's eyes. She sobbed, "I'm sorry."

He made a low grunt of pain, like an animal mortally wounded. "This is where it ends. There's nothing left of me but this miserable carcass I drag about."

Giselle thought that was a little melodramatic—the cheap scotch talking. "Where is she?"

"Where is who?"

"Miranda's body. Have they buried her?"

"Not yet. They're still going through the formalities."

Giselle mopped her face and sat up. She pushed the medical cart away, angry suddenly. "You're going to leave her there? In that place where she was robbed of everything?"

"I think it's what she would have wanted."

"No, definitely not. She would have wanted to come home." With a scornful look, she ordered, "Get off that deathbed. You haven't earned it."

Dr. Redman responded with the shaken calm of a man who had witnessed his own emotional disintegration only to be faced with a loose end. Dazedly, he asked, "What makes you so certain?"

"I painted her portrait. I looked at every photograph you have. I saw a woman who could be joyful and confident in her adventure because she was secure in her roots. Your daughter was deeply connected to the world around her. Those pictures…many of them were taken here. She kept coming back, don't you see? She didn't have to, she wanted to. That's how I know what she'd want now."

His shoulders slumped. He lowered his head to his hands.

"Bring her home," Giselle said. "Do this one last thing for her, not for you." She stood up and collected the syringes from the medical trolley.

Like he'd just jumped off a moving train and was finding his legs, Dr. Redman staggered as he moved away from the operating table.

"I made some coffee." Giselle marched him out of the room.

"Thank you," he said when she handed him a mug.

They both leaned back against the kitchen counter.

"I'll bring you something to eat later," Giselle said. "You have a lot to think about."

He kissed her on the cheek. "You're very kind."

The confession. A coveted badge of honor for all detectives, the closest they came to an art form, Dale thought. Some of hers felt like poetry in motion, or so she claimed during the beer-drinking rites that took place after these milestones.

She sat down opposite the individual she and Babineaux had picked up early in the afternoon. Not the usual collar. This guy had calmly walked into Charles' Southern Style Kitchen on 125th and Lenox, and ordered oxtails and gravy. While it was not unusual for the regular clientele to share counter space with a stranger covered in blood, they were not used to seeing a man of the cloth in that condition. Hence the 911 call.

Babineaux has already taken a run at him while Dale was interviewing a hooker about the bodega killing. Turned out, this witness had been blowing some john behind the store and saw the killer's feet as he ran past. They now had a good description of shoes that could belong to anyone.

Dale, however, was not feeling discouraged. She'd been looking forward to the next interview, certain they were going to get results in this fresh case. Already, they had bloody clothing in an evidence bag. DNA up the yazoo. A situation like this commanded optimism.

She began cheerfully. "Father Dunaway—"

"That's Pastor. I used to be a priest. I left the church for the sacrament of marriage."

Dale inspected him closely. His cheeks were a fish-belly tone and his hands were probably clammy. He kept pressing them together like there was something sandwiched between them other than his own damp, chubby flesh.

"Pastor, you were telling Detective Babineaux earlier about your mission."

"I operate a faith-based initiative aimed at the transformation of sinners and the reclamation of their immortal souls."

Funded by the know-nothings on Capitol Hill, needless to say. Dale exchanged a quick glance with Babineaux, who signaled for her to run the interrogation.

"There's plenty of room for improvement around here, Pastor," she remarked approvingly.

He said, "My calling takes me to places of perversion that would frighten most people."

Dale gave a sage nod. "The New York Sports Clubs on W. 125th Street being one of them." The NYSC Harlem was not quite as gay as David Barton or the Equinox, but Dale wouldn't want the cleaning contract.

Dunaway drained the Pepsi from his paper cup and asked, "Where's my dog been taken?"

"To the shelter. He's fine."

"I keep him muzzled," Dunaway said.

"I'd like to discuss the blood on your clothes," Dale said. "You don't have injuries. Did you encounter an injured person some time today who may need to see a doctor?"

"I explained to the other detective that I was accosted by a homeless gentleman near Starbucks. He looked like he had been in a fight. That's how the blood came to be on my clothing."

Dale read the report. A few residents reported seeing Dunaway wandering along W. 125th Street with his pit bull. No one saw a bloody homeless man, and he hadn't presented himself at any hospital in the area. He would have been on foot, or maybe he took a bus.

"Maybe you can find the blood in your database," Dunaway suggested.

Dale greeted this misapprehension with a show of interest, recognizing that they had their first opening. As an interrogation progressed, offenders usually tried to find out how much the police knew. A delicate balancing act ensued. The only way to verify a confession was to hold back information only the offender would know. Yet to get the confession, it was essential to build a rapport.

Dale often devoted hours to establishing a bond with a suspect, keeping him talking, trying to read him so she could adjust her approach. Eventually, she would see subtle shifts as an offender moved from outright denial to hints that he was there or saw something, to an admission of involvement and then the full details of the confession. All the while, she would keep the suspect talking.

There was nothing quite like eating hamburgers with a man who'd killed his pregnant wife so he could set up house with the babysitter. Sympathizing over his dilemma. Remarking on the difficulties of getting rid of a body. Dale felt dirty and sad in most interrogations, listening to the unthinkable and hiding her emotions.

Sensing a readiness to talk in Dunaway, she exploited the opening he'd provided. "That blood belongs to a convicted felon, Pastor. That's why I'm asking you all these questions. He's a wanted man."

The silence was electrifying. Dunaway, a man of small, round stature, grew a few inches in his chair. "Wanted for what?"

Dale rolled the dice. "I'm not free to disclose that information as we have criminal charges pending. However, I can say that certain crimes are considered especially heinous by the NYPD."

He watched television. "Sex crimes?"

She gave a noncommittal shrug, but displayed a flash of feminine revulsion.

Dunaway reacted with chivalrous consternation. "I've always said the NYPD should have more concern for women in your job. There's no reason why you should have to be involved in cases that are deeply offensive."

"I'm sickened on a daily basis," Dale confided in a low voice. "I have nightmares."

"And you should be protected." Dunaway stared up at the ceiling and addressed the monitor. "This is immoral. You should not expose your female officers to sexual perverts."

Dale sighed. "Nothing will ever change. It's an impossible struggle."

"Not if we place our trust in Jesus," Dunaway said. "My life was turned around. I used to work for the IRS. Now I have my own church and I make a difference every day."

"I believe you." Dale allowed a trace of admiration to seep into her tone.

"The man you're talking about was a deviant," Dunaway announced with an air of benevolence. "He offended my Lord."

"And the people of New York," Dale added.

She knew what was happening behind the one-way mirror; she could almost feel the sudden charge in the atmosphere as everyone tensed and listened more acutely. Dunaway had just admitted to contact with a probable victim. He was using the past tense, starting to justify his own actions. The confession had begun.

Like most offenders, the man before her would hold back little things that could make him look bad. There was always an angle, a bid for understanding. Dunaway saw himself as a defender of values and a man who respected women. The targets of his loathing were almost certainly gays and prostitutes. He would blame the victim for the crime, and Dale would encourage him to do so.

She sipped some water like she was taking a break and her guard was lowered. "I'll tell you what makes me sick to my stomach," she said like she couldn't wait to share her secret views with a man who would applaud them. "Perverts that come in here making complaints, wasting police time. A nice college student goes missing, probably kidnapped, but what are we doing? Looking for a guy some queer claims raped him. In my opinion, you live that lifestyle, you have it coming."

"God hates the sin, but loves the sinner," Dunaway reminded her.

"Well, I'm not God."

This brought tears of laughter to his eyes. He got hysterical, laying his head on the table and snorting noisily.

Dale twisted the phony wedding ring she wore when she questioned suspects. Pressing on with the homophobic bonding, she said, "I know the first thing I'd do if I was God." She cast a nervous look around.

Dunaway raised his head and wiped his face, agog. "I promise I won't tell a soul."

"They would be off the streets tomorrow. Mothers would be able to walk their children anywhere in New York City without fearing what could happen." She smiled at him, as if she was seeking his approval. "What about you? What would you do if you had the power?"

"Wipe them off the map," he said.

"I suppose, being an attractive man, you've had your share of harassment." Dale offered world-weary empathy. "I can hardly stand to think about it…the filthy, disgusting things they do to each other."

He got angry. "I placed an advertisement once. For companionship. I met someone I became fond off." His high-pitched voice wavered. "I was thinking about marriage."

Dale nodded like she was hearing a nice story that was supposed to have a happy ending, but possibly wouldn't. Cautiously, she said, "She must have been special."

"Special!"

"For you to think of marriage."

"She was special alright. I was conned by an expert, a man pretending to be a woman."

"Terrible," Dale said. "Was there a financial motivation?"

"No, it was nothing more than filthy sexual perversion. I was drawn into a vile encounter. That's when I discovered the deception."

"You must have been so shocked. What on earth did you do? How did you protect yourself?"

"I kicked him where it hurts and set Baldric on him."

"Your pit-bull terrier?"

"Taught him the lesson of a lifetime." He made a defeated hand gesture. "There, I just confessed to beating up a transvestite. Go ahead. Place me under arrest."

"Did this happen today?" Dale asked. Without waiting for an answer, she continued, "Because maybe you won't be in as much trouble as you think. The man whose blood we found on your suit and shirt is on our files as a sex offender."

She waited for this phony good news to sink in.

Dunaway peered across at her with an impatient expression, his beady blue eyes red rimmed. "No, that was another occasion. Today I had to defend myself against a different creep. "

Dale touched her throat.

"They're everywhere," he said. "Like cockroaches. The only answer is…extermination."

❖

"Who is she?" Babineaux asked two hours later while Dale was trying to finish her report.

Dunaway had been charged with killing a transsexual

prostitute called Madonna. He had taken the detectives to Riverside Drive, not far from the Grinnell apartment building everyone photographed. Her body was dumped along a popular river walk. She'd been bitten by a dog and her slinky dress was covered in blood.

"Who is who?" Dale asked.

Babineaux rolled his eyes. "The hot date."

"You tell me."

"You forgot to drink your coffee this morning. You're on the phone with a stupid look on your face. You're not drinking tonight, after *that* confession. Do I look like a retard?"

"I'm tired."

"No kidding. You look like you haven't slept in a year." He sighed. "Some people have all the luck."

"You're married with kids," Dale said. "Marcia has better things to do than walk around in a French-maid outfit."

"I wish I'd never showed you that fucking Web site."

"Don't kid yourself that I'm the one having a good time. You've got a family. Make the most of it."

"Vegas," Babineaux mused. "That's the deal. A week on my own, doing—"

"I don't want to hear it."

Babineaux was all hot air and they both knew it. If he ever went to Vegas, Marcia would be at his side. Dale wasn't sure why he needed to pretend otherwise, but that was how married cops talked. Normally she shrugged it off, but today she wasn't in the mood. She felt jaded and dirty. All she could think about was taking a shower and sitting in a quiet room. She wanted to see Giselle. She wanted a sweet woman on her lap, smelling good and chattering about nothing.

She wanted to connect with something good and real and wholesome.

CHAPTER TWELVE

Between Harlem and heaven, the Isaiah Owens' Funeral Home offered a compassionate and elegant respite for countless grieving families and for the deceased themselves. Abiding earnestly by his mortuary's motto, "Where Beauty Softens Your Grief," Mr. Owens was known by some as "the artful undertaker" and others as "The Prophet." Giselle wasn't sure how he came by the latter soubriquet, but one thing was certain: he could accurately predict the potential of wounded, bruised, and misshapen bodies to look fabulous in an open coffin.

In Miranda's case, confronted with an assortment of bones, hair, and torn clothing scraps, he said, "Not even a superb embalmer and restorative artist, such as myself, could transform this poor child. It's heartbreaking. I know it, Dr. Redman. But you got to go with the closed coffin."

"That's what I thought." Dr. Redman ran a thin silk handkerchief across his brow. He had the trembles. He hadn't been drinking since his thwarted date with the Grim Reaper several weeks before.

As Giselle had hoped, getting Miranda's body back to the USA had been an epic feat, requiring diplomatic phone calls, conversations in several languages, and a bribe that had cleaned out most of the cash he had squirreled away. Miranda's funeral would consume the rest. Dr. Redman didn't seem unduly bothered by this state of affairs. Apart from the trembling hands, he was as serene as she'd ever known him to be.

Still concerned for his reputation, Mr. Owens, a man of stature and flair, said, "I must be honest, sir. I don't recommend the postmortem portrait either."

Giselle glanced around the walls. Countless formal portraits of beautifully coiffed and dressed deceased hung as a testament to the cosmetologist's art. These impressive studies were the work of Elizabeth Heyert, a photographer who aimed to chronicle the vanishing funeral customs of Harlem. Giselle was struck by the sensitivity of the portraits and by the way Mr. Owens had dressed and presented each person, in readiness to meet God. Somehow the photographs eliminated melancholy, yet still left room for grief. She found that intriguing.

Giselle wondered if it would be in bad taste to ask Mr. Owens if she could paint a portrait of one of his clients at some future time. She decided to say nothing today. There was a funeral service to plan and Dr. Redman was splashing out. Miranda was going to have the works: a white coffin, a jazz band, and a party catered by Miss Maude. Doctors Without Borders was sending a delegation, and there were rumors that the Clintons might make an appearance because Miranda's story had been on television. Anderson Cooper from CNN had sent an advance scouting party, and this decision had all the cable networks making inquiries. As a consequence, the Crips and the Bloods were talking about another day of reconciliation. They needed to prove that they hadn't gone away now that their traditional territories were being overrun by white refugees fleeing the high cost of living Downtown.

Dr. Redman seemed to be coping well with the sudden media exposure. Giselle hoped he wasn't just putting on a front and biding his time for another suicide attempt. She had emptied every bottle of alcohol in his apartment down the sink, and had hired a maid service to clean the place. To her surprise, he'd acquiesced to this high-handed management without a whimper. He was even going to AA meetings, although he explained that, as a business strategy; he was casting the net a little wider. Once he stopped shaking, he planned to perform more discount face-lifts and undersell the other unlicensed surgeon who did most of these procedures, Dr. Hacker of Washington Heights.

Dr. Redman was, as he put it, "Fed up with mopping up after that butcher." The way he was talking, it seemed his lethal-injection plan was merely a bad memory. Giselle hoped so. She didn't have enough friends to lose one.

❖

"What do you think?" Giselle led Dale into an airy studio that had been gutted and refinished in white. Canvases occupied the walls, and a freestanding central workbench was covered in brushes and tubes of paint. At the far end an area was set up for models to change and sit.

"It's ideal." Dale tried to show enthusiasm.

Giselle's face was pink with pleasure. She was all but dancing around the room. "I have the lease for a year. Francesca says by that time I should be able to support myself fully from my work."

"Wonderful." Dale was about ready to barf if she heard that name again. She hadn't met Giselle's "patron" yet and she wanted to be wholeheartedly supportive, but Sandy's glib remarks fluttered like Post-its in the back of her mind. Rich. Closeted. Obsessed with the fine arts. *Adores* Giselle.

"She doesn't want me to exhibit yet. She feels I should study in Europe next year."

"Europe." It wasn't the moon. Dale had been saving for an overseas trip now that she'd finished the most expensive renovations to her condo. Assuming she could reach a sane compromise with Penelope before there were more legal bills to pay, she could plan a visit while Giselle was studying.

Dale reminded herself that she had no right to feel resentful about the sweeping changes in Giselle's humdrum life since the advent of Francesca Larson a month ago. Giselle was her own agent and owed it to herself to develop her natural gift. Dale wasn't an art aficionado, by any stretch of the imagination, but even she could see a haunting quality in her lover's work. When she set aside her personal discomfort with the idea of unsuspecting, innocent Giselle being the protégée of a wealthy lesbian, she was truly happy for her.

"I can't wait to show Mom," Giselle crowed. "She thinks my painting is a waste of time."

"You should have a party here," Dale suggested without thinking.

As soon as the words fell from her lips she wished she could take them back. Did she really want to see Giselle hanging off the arm of her new best friend, being introduced to people with Park Avenue addresses who viewed artists as a special class of fashionable pet?

"Francesca thinks so, too," Giselle said happily. "She's already making arrangements. All I have to do is e-mail a guest list to her personal assistant."

Naturally Francesca had everything under control. Dale should have guessed. Aggravated, she said, "I'm proud of you, Giselle. This is big. One day you'll be famous, and I'll be telling people how I used to know you back when you lived in a walk-up in Harlem."

Giselle turned wounded dark eyes on her. "One of the many notches on your belt?"

"That's not what I meant."

"You don't have to explain yourself. I know the score." The cynical edge was at odds with her clasped hands and discreet lip-chewing.

Dale closed her hands over Giselle's wrists and said, "I made a tactless, stupid comment. I'm sorry."

She parted the clasped hands and drew Giselle into an embrace. Here, of all the special moments during the past weeks, was an I Love You waiting to happen. Dale even had the feelings to go with it, if she wanted to interpret her messy responses to

Giselle as "love." She refrained. Some people tossed the L-word around after a second date. They could acquire the same instant devotion to a pair of jeans or a hit song, and lose the attachment just as fast. Their emotional repertoire was an all-you-can-eat fast-food buffet, plenty to choose from and nothing to savor.

She ran her hands over Giselle's now-familiar curves, inhaled her ginger and old-rose scent, and fought the urge to fall on her knees in front of her. Lift her skirt. Tear off her panties. Part the wet red hair so she could feast at will. Her desire for Giselle ran at a constant high. She went through the motions of life and work, drunk with its intensity, hanging out for the next opportunity to slake her thirst. They could make love for hours. She could explore every concealed crevice, demanding all Giselle could give, and still she was unsatisfied. Still she glimpsed in her lover a maddening, elusive self she couldn't touch.

Right now, however, Giselle's body was speaking to her, summoning her to the terrain they'd claimed for themselves. Dale lowered her head. Her mouth came to rest on Giselle's. Damp, warm air clung to her face as they shared one breath after the next, each fraught with anticipation. Giselle's tongue touched Dale's top lip where it was most sensitive. They both shivered. Their hearts pounded roughly against one another, their bodies tensed.

Dale knew this wordless dance well. She leaned in and let Giselle know, with a slow grind of the hips, that she was wanted. Giselle linked her hands tightly behind Dale's neck. The swift arch of Giselle's back brought them hard into contact. Dale cupped her hands beneath Giselle's ass and hitched her up. Giselle's legs curled around her, and Dale walked them back a few paces until they hit a wall.

There, she drove herself against Giselle, pressure building. Finally, they kissed. Slid down. Bit and licked and grabbed. Dale tore Giselle's panties off and threw them aside. The bare floor crunched her knees. She shook off her jacket and spread it on the wood. Giselle shuffled over. Dale pushed her onto her back and opened her legs wide so she could look all she wanted.

She said, "No one gets to have you this way, but me."

Somewhere a door slammed. They froze. Dale could only interpret the metallic thuds and creaks because she knew the sounds of a person approaching in an unfamiliar building. She pulled Giselle's skirt down to cover her pale thighs.

"Giselle?" The studio door needed oil.

They scrambled up. Dale brushed herself off.

"I know I'm early." Sandy stepped around the corner. Her smile slid. Her eyes dropped to the jacket at Dale's feet.

Then they were all staring at the filmy, frilly ball of damp white lace a few feet away. Sandy picked the panties up between forefinger and thumb and held them out. "Notice how I'm not saying a word?"

Dale zipped herself up.

Giselle plucked her underclothing from Sandy's hand.

"Great space. Good to see you're already taking full advantage." Sandy wandered toward the windows.

Giselle stammered, "I was going to tell you before."

This lame assertion did nothing to thaw Sandy's expression. "You're grown adults. What you do in your spare time is none of my business."

Her words had just enough sting to make Giselle wring her hands, a difficult move while she was still clutching the panties.

Impatiently, Sandy said, "Girl, go do something with those."

Giselle fled, leaving Dale in the position she'd so far avoided: what to tell Sandy, and how to tell it. She got straight to the point. "We're sleeping together and I'm serious about her. It's been going on for a month."

Sandy greeted these rash words with grave-eyed calm. "That's a giant step in the right direction."

Dale said, "You were singing a different tune the last time we shared on the subject of my romantic failures."

"Yes, and if I remember correctly, you were planning another fuck-and-run. What happened?"

"Jesus, I don't know." Dale felt like she'd been flattened by a semi.

"Are you in love?"

Dale took a moment to allow her thoughts to take shape. "I'm starting to think I'd like to be."

Sandy smiled. "Mnhmn."

"She's quite something."

"I know," Sandy said. "That's why I want her to find the right person. Is that you?"

Dale wasn't sure how to answer. "Maybe it wasn't me six months ago. Sandy, I haven't felt this way in a long time. I'm trying to give it some room, so I'll know if it's for real."

"Have you told her how you feel?"

Dale laughed. "I'm waiting for the other shoe to fall."

"Always the optimist."

"How about you?" Dale asked, remembering that Sandy had been talking about dating a woman recently. "Anything doing?"

"I met someone, but it's one-sided. I'm crazy about her. She's lukewarm about me. "

"I find that hard to believe." Was there really a moron out there who would not reciprocate love and adoration from *this* woman?

Sandy shrugged. "We've had this conversation."

"The one about settling?" Dale joined her by the windows.

"It's not that she won't date me. Or sleep with me. Or live with me." Sandy sounded defeated. "But she doesn't want *me*. She wants a wife. It could be anyone."

"Give me her address and I'll go 'round there and beat some sense into her."

"That's what I love about you. Your finesse." Sandy tucked her hand in Dale's arm. "So you see the problem. Knowing all of that, knowing I'd just be furniture, do I settle?"

"Ouch."

"It could be worse, I guess." Sandy's voice was strained. "I could settle for someone I *don't* love."

"Actually, that might be easier." Dale knew which one she would choose. "If you're not in love, you can't be hurt. You're not vulnerable. You get to keep your self-respect. In the long run, that's what counts."

Sandy lowered her head to Dale's shoulder. "I warned you off Giselle because I thought it could only be one-sided, and I know how much that hurts."

"I'm not going to hurt her." Dale smiled ironically to herself. It was quite something to realize that if something went wrong now, she would be miserable.

They stood there for a moment, then they both looked around.

"She's taking her time." Dale strode to the studio door.

"I hear something." Sandy led the way up a flight of stairs to a door marked Roof.

They stepped out into the pungent stillness of early summer. Giselle had her back to them. She was on her hands and knees, reaching into a hole in the decaying masonry around a disused chimney. Next to her were two writhing kittens.

"Oh, my God," Sandy gasped.

Giselle gave a start and swung her head around. Her face was filthy. "Can you two find a box? I'm getting the last one out now, and once I have all of them, the mother cat will follow."

Dale grinned. She'd heard about the animal-rescue habit from the alcoholic doctor in the apartment below Giselle's.

Sandy slapped her on the shoulder. "She's all yours."

❖

Dale opened the hefty handmade-paper envelope that had arrived in the squad room by special delivery. At first, when someone yelled for her to sign for a letter, she'd thought she was being served. But that would have been too easy. Because Dale had done something to piss God off, she didn't receive a pissant summons; what she held in her hand was the latest bombshell from Penelope. The invitation was made out to "Dale Porter (and male partner, if desired.)"

Dale supposed she should be thankful the envelope did not contain polonium, although who knew? The effects weren't immediately apparent. She said a loud, "Fuck you."

"What did I do?" Babineaux bleated. "You don't have to come. I can tell Marcia you're busy."

Dale rolled her eyes. "I don't know what you're talking about."

"July fourth. Barbecue *chez* Babineaux."

Dale slapped her head. In the domestic furor around the opening party for Giselle's studio, an event that had taken on its own scary Francesca-driven momentum, she had completely forgotten the annual Babineaux shindig was just days away. Now, as if she didn't have enough to think about, her crazy sister had invited her to the wedding-anniversary party she and Carl could not afford to throw. Where in the world were they finding the money to pay for it?

Dale felt sick. She told Babineaux, "I'm coming to the barbecue, and I'm bringing Giselle."

Her partner grinned. "Hot and heavy now, huh? You planning a trip to Vermont?"

Dale said, "The day that looks like happening, you'll be the first to know." She paced around her desk a few times and said, "Cover for me, would you, pal? I have to go out."

❖

Mrs. Porter was a small, pink-cheeked older woman with her white hair crimped in a tight perm. When she saw Giselle, she said, "Slut."

Which was how Giselle felt after spending the entire of

the unexpected drive to Tarrytown lasciviously cruising Dale's body. She liked when Dale came 'round to the apartment on an errand in the middle of a shift. Seeing her in her working clothes, wearing a shoulder holster, all businesslike and unwilling to make out, made Giselle want to suck her just the way she liked. And sometimes that was exactly what happened. But not today.

Today, flirting had got her nowhere. She hadn't been able to provoke more than a vague smile with suggestive remarks about touching herself while Dale watched. She had pointed out that Dale wouldn't have to smell of pussy when she went back to work, but apparently that was the least of Dale's concerns. Now that they were here, Giselle could see why.

Dale said, "Mom, this is my girlfriend, Giselle Truelove."

Mrs. Porter glared at Giselle and asked, "Where's Penelope?"

"Oh, for Christ's sake!" Dale stormed out of the room followed by the housekeeper, Ophelia Williams.

This statuesque older African-American woman knew her well enough to yell at her. Giselle could hear them going at it.

Ophelia: "Even when she was a youngster, Mrs. Avaryss was a spoiled, sulky, selfish, manipulative bitch. And that's on a good day. You never saw her for who she is. Never! She played you. She played me. She played Miss Laurel. And she sure played that poor fool she married."

Dale: "She's taking this to court. It's costing me more money than I have."

Ophelia: "You so messed up, you ain't thinking. Fighting her, that's the *wrong* thing to do."

A long silence, then: "Okay, what the fuck do you suggest, because I'm fresh out of ideas."

"Watch your mouth."

"I'm sorry. Oh, God." Loud sobs.

Shocked, Giselle lurched from her chair and ran toward the small parlor a few doors from the main living area. This was, she decided, Ophelia's personal parlor in the main house. The room was homey and busy, with a large velvet painting of Jesus on one wall and ornately framed family pictures choking every inch of flat surface. Ophelia loved her son and his children with a passion, yet she'd spent almost all her adult life looking after some other woman's family. How weird was that?

And how weird was Dale, bent over with her face buried in her hands, completely losing it? She and Ophelia sat next to each other on the sofa. Ophelia's big arm looked exactly the right size for Dale's shoulders. She hugged her and rocked her like she was a child.

Not sure how to fit into this picture, or whether to try, Giselle knelt down in front of Dale and kissed whatever she could get to. Dale's shirt collar. Her head. Her knees. When no one pushed her away, she asked, "What's going on?"

Dale had only told her a few sketchy details about her older sister Penelope, who wanted their mother to go into assisted living, which on first impression didn't seem unreasonable.

Ophelia replied, with a hint of condescension, "Family business." She wiggled a little in her floral cotton dress and checked the buttons at her neckline. Giselle had the impression she was embarrassed on Dale's behalf.

"I know this has nothing to do with me, but maybe I can help. If you tell me what's going on." Giselle glanced around, asking politely, "Is that your son, Mrs. Williams? He's very handsome. I see the resemblance."

"Giselle paints portraits," Dale said, as if this made her a connoisseur of good looks. Her face was no longer buried in her hands, but she was very pale and the shadows around her eyes unusually pronounced.

Giselle had noticed them before, but she hadn't realized that they were about sorrow and stress. Dale's weariness from work coupled with sleep deprivation had taken a toll on her. Giselle felt partly to blame for the ill effects. They stayed up having sex all night, too many nights in a row.

It was easy for Giselle. She didn't have to rush out the door at six a.m. But Dale was getting short-tempered, and she'd told Giselle she sometimes went to sleep in a back room at the station. None of this helped her emotional state; Giselle could see that now. Neither did locking in her feelings. It was unhealthy.

She squeezed Dale's knee. "Whatever the problem, there's always a solution. People just get stuck."

"That's what I was telling her," Ophelia said.

"Do you have any ideas?" Giselle asked.

Ophelia nodded. "I sure do."

Dale sat up and straightened her clothing. Her long fingers toyed with the neck of her shirt. She took a deep breath. "I'm listening."

"Miss Laurel, she's mentally incompetent just like Mrs. Avaryss says. That's what the judge is going to think. You got no chance, Dale. Look at her."

"So I should just give up?"

Ophelia rolled her eyes. "No, here's what you do. You got to make that judge appoint *you* as the guardian, not your greedy-ass sister."

Dale frowned. "Why didn't I think of that?"

"Because she's your big sister and you think she's the boss."

"But, you're the boss." Dale grinned wanly.

"You sure got that right."

"It's a good idea," Giselle said. "Then you're not fighting her. You're letting her do the legal work for you."

"Yeah, I can beat her at her own game." Dale threw an arm around Ophelia and hugged her close. "I'll tell my attorney."

"What you paying *him* for, when you can come here for your good advice."

Dale kissed Ophelia on the cheek. "I'll remember that for next time." Her expression altered and she was all business suddenly. "This can work. I need to get all the information so the judge can see Penelope is financially motivated and Mom will get better care if I'm in charge." Her mouth became taut. "I'm going to hang her using every piece of rope she's ever given me."

"That's right." Ophelia nodded.

Dale dropped an expensive invitation on the table. "Check this out. It arrived today."

Giselle waited for Ophelia to read the few lines of fancy print. Noisy sound effects ensued.

"Shoot. She's lost her mind," Ophelia said. "There's my other idea. Why don't you file a motion to have Mrs. Avaryss declared mentally incompetent? They gonna hear how she spent a thousand dollars on thirty bottles of nail polish. What do you think they'll say? Crazy or just too stupid to breathe?"

Dale laughed. At first the sound was a weak gurgle that came from her throat, then she was howling. Ophelia rocked herself and clutched her sides. Giselle figured there was more to that joke than she could comprehend. But she would get it when she got to know Dale's family.

CHAPTER THIRTEEN

Francesca Larson ran a possessive hand over the naked canvas of Giselle's shoulder. "Come meet Victor Bradley. He's interested in one of your cityscapes. He's a developer. I've been advising him on his collection."

Giselle cast a helpless look at Dale and vanished into the crowd with Francesca's hand resting in the small of her back. The studio was packed with people dressed in black. A ritzy catering firm plied the guests with mediocre wine and tiny finger food. Francesca had hired the Danny Mixon Trio to provide an authentic Harlem atmosphere. After a foot-stomping warm-up set, they'd switched to smooth jazz. A few couples were dancing.

Sandy came over. She was wearing a very plain midnight blue cocktail dress.

"Hot dress," Dale said.

Sandy returned the compliment. "You look extremely fuckable, yourself."

"Dark rings of exhaustion. Who knew they could be a turn-on?"

"Want to dance?" Sandy asked.

"I'm not much of a dancer."

"I know. We can just mooch."

They moved into an idle rhythm. Sandy pointed toward a group of people gathered around Francesca. "Giselle wants to lick you. She's staring."

Dale met her lover's eyes and pasted on a look of enjoyment, like she was thrilled by this circus. "I don't think I've ever seen so many pretentious people in one room."

"You don't get to many art openings, do you?"

"I can live with the disappointment."

"Quite a mix," Sandy said, identifying the various cliques circling like shoals of fish. "East Village dykes. Oil executives with bloated expense accounts. Queer-as-fuck art critics."

They moved into a closer embrace, and Dale was surprised at herself as Sandy's lissome body slid against her own. She was holding a woman who drew constant predatory glances from various quarters of the room, but she could think only of her lover. She watched strangers inspect Giselle, touch her, drop their heads close to hers to listen to her. Everyone seemed large and dark and looming, gathered in their black cocktail plumage like hungry crows around a meal they would soon tear apart.

Dale wanted to rescue her, a foolish idea. Giselle had spoken nonstop about this event ever since the date was set. Francesca had invited two other artists to share the spotlight. Dale had to admit, the woman knew what she was doing. She had chosen several of Giselle's paintings she thought would whet appetites. These were exhibited alongside works that were in stark contrast. Among these were a couple of large canvases by a hot young superstar called Zack Mack, who had a brief career as a porn star before Francesca discovered him.

As she and Sandy inched their way around the room in a half-hearted two-step, Dale took in one of his paintings, a huge confusing montage of photograph fragments. Pink telephone receivers drifted like flotsam on this debris. The faces of four girls with green halos glowed pale and bright in the center. Each wore an identical bored expression. The title of this masterpiece was "Phone Sex Is Boring."

Dale overheard someone harping on about this "raw statement by rebellious youth," and the "indictment of a value-free consumer culture." The artist appeared to be doing okay.

The price tag was $30,000, and one of Francesca's flunkies was taking names for a list of prospective buyers. The unlucky ones who missed out on getting one of Mr. Mack's paintings tonight would be considered for future works.

The other protégé Francesca had chosen was an Iraq veteran called something like Todd or Bud, who was making a living painting the battle dramas he'd survived. Earlier, Giselle had explained her patron's thinking along these lines: "His dispassionate photorealism and dramatic representational approach creates a sharp contrast with the mystery and emotionality of my portraiture. His presence draws in mature executives who don't know much about art, but like war movies."

Evidently these well-heeled captains of industry were willing to spend $20,000 to buy one of his paintings, and they also wanted their pictures taken with an artist who was a decorated war hero.

The early crowd had thinned out, making room for new arrivals. Giselle kept staring toward the door, doubtless waiting for her mother to make her entrance. Nashleigh Whittaker had flown in from Barbados for the event and was bringing the Italian fiancé Dale had heard all about. She probably intended to arrive fashionably late, keeping Giselle on edge, worried that she wouldn't come at all. Their relationship was a little rocky, Dale had gleaned, much the same as her own with Laurel.

A shaft of irritation stiffened her back, reminding her that she was stressed beyond measure by her family situation. Ophelia's theory was that Penelope intended to wear them all down until she got her way. Unlike Dale, she had time to make trouble, and she'd made it quite clear that she had nothing to lose. She didn't have a sentimental attachment to the Tarrytown house or care whether their mother did. She frequently pointed out that Laurel would soon forget who they both were, and claimed they'd both suffered because Laurel was a lousy mother when they were kids. As for their bond as sisters, apparently Penelope didn't give a damn.

Dale found that fact incredibly hurtful. She couldn't believe what her sister was putting the family through. If she had her way, their mother would end up in an institution; Ophelia would be homeless and have to move in with her son. The house, with its generations of family memories, would be owned by strangers. And for what? An anniversary party to celebrate the marriage she wanted to end, shared with the husband she despised?

Dale took stock of her situation. She had lost her father, was losing her mother, and had no meaningful, loving connection with her sister. The thought made her sick at heart. Without family, not much else mattered. Upset, she tried to catch Giselle's eye, suddenly yearning for an affirmation that they mattered to each other more than either of them had verbally acknowledged. That had to change. Dale wanted Giselle to know where she stood. And she wanted to know if Giselle felt the same way.

How much longer would this event drag on? The assistant taking names for Giselle's list seemed busy, which Dale surmised was a good thing. Francesca had informed them as they prepared for the evening that portraiture was not "hot" at the moment, but that good portrait artists were in high demand all the same. America had minted a new wave of millionaires over the past decade. Many of these technology-boom tycoons were nerds trying to assume the mantle of wealth like it belonged. Part of that process involved sitting for a boardroom portrait to replace the ones of them airborne at the skateboarding alley and shaking hands with Steve Jobs. So far, Francesca had secured expressions of interest from three of these customers.

"Did you plan this?" Dale asked as she and Sandy drifted out of their feeble dance and started wandering around the perimeters of the room.

"Honestly?" Sandy seemed embarrassed. "No. I was trying to fix Giselle up with a woman who would make her feel special. I thought Francesca would be nice about her paintings and that would boost her ego. But this? No."

"Because she's not that good as an artist?"

"Oh, please. Who can say what's 'good' anymore? Do you

seriously think most of this crowd has a clue?" Sandy laughed. "The reason people hang around Francesca is that they think *she* knows. In art, there's a lot of money to be made if you *know* who's going to be hot in ten years' time."

Dale watched one of the millionaire nerds tear his iPod away from his ear so he could hit on an art critic. The woman stared in puzzled horror, like he had just emerged from primeval slime. Dale's gaze drifted to Giselle once more and she decided she'd seen enough. Francesca's hand was constantly on some part of Giselle. Her shoulder. Her arm. Her cheek. Her arm brushed past Giselle's breasts as she shook hands with whomever. Dale tried to tell herself that she was reading too much into mannerisms that were applied universally, except that this was not so.

Francesca, while giving the impression of warmth, guarded her personal space carefully, keeping people at arm's length. Only Giselle stood within her aura. They made quite a couple, Francesca very cool and elegant in her black suit and stark white shirt; Giselle moving like a lovely nymph in emerald green, her hair glowing copper-red. Dale could see that Francesca was aware of their visual appeal and loved every minute; she was the type who enjoyed letting people speculate.

For a woman supposedly closeted, she sure knew how to make a statement about her sexuality. Her conscious gender-bending made her the center of attention. The choice of emphatically masculine attire emphasized her classic female beauty. Dale thought she would probably be a fascinating lover. Her self-possession was alluring. She was one of the few women Dale had ever encountered who could invoke a submissive response. Normally, Dale would have been open to exploring her own unsettling reactions. She recognized that Francesca was a highly refined Dominant, much more subtle than most. An encounter with her would be quite something.

Dale felt uneasy. Would Giselle be drawn by that energy? If Francesca made her an offer, would Giselle be tempted to explore a more ritualized dynamic? Would she be curious? Dale watched the dance taking place between them and saw a collector tying silk to the leg of a butterfly. Francesca would not make a direct move unless she was certain the path was clear; she was old school. Ten years older than Dale and light-years away in terms of the lives they led. She had so much to offer Giselle that Dale knew she should think seriously about walking away.

"Dale?" Sandy stepped back from her, and Dale realized she had lost all concentration. "I think I'll hit the bar."

"Go ahead," Dale said. "I need to talk to someone." She moved through the crowd and edged her way past the fashion victims clustered in Francesca's orbit.

Giselle's pupils dilated and her mouth parted softly. She gazed at Dale like she was the only woman in the room and, with a polite "excuse me," moved away from Francesca. She walked in step at Dale's side until they found a shadowed corner behind the long central divider where most of the works for sale were on display.

"What do you think?" she asked Dale excitedly. "Isn't it amazing?"

"Francesca has been very good to you. Have you seen your list?"

Giselle lowered her voice. "I've sold two paintings. Six thousand dollars each. Can you believe that?"

Dale said, "I like your paintings better than that Mack kid's, and they're lining up to pay thirty grand for one of his."

"He's very creative," Giselle said. "His work makes a statement."

"Yeah, a statement that he can't paint a face at all, so he paints the same one over and over and pretends it's supposed to look like a zombie. And he can't paint a proper background with trees or whatever, so he cuts up photographs his friends take. Fuck me, what a genius."

Giselle stifled a giggle. She ran a hand down Dale's shirt and said, "I wish we were all alone. I've been missing you. Two days apart while I was working on all this…I am…Well, you know."

"Tell me about it." Dale's throat went dry as Giselle tugged playfully at her belt.

"I hope we can escape soon."

"Somehow I think Francesca has other plans," Dale said. "Remember, you're one of the stars. You can't sneak away from your own party to make love."

A broad, mischievous smile lit Giselle's face. These days, she was less self-conscious and didn't hide her mouth when she was amused. "There's always the roof."

Dale was tempted. Incredibly so. She'd been swollen and throbbing all evening, simultaneously annoyed by Francesca and turned on by the sight of Giselle in her flimsy green cocktail dress, expanses of milky pale skin drawing stares all 'round. She was on the brink of seizing Giselle by the hand and escaping from the crush, when Giselle waved at someone. Dr. Redman had just walked in the door. Dale was relieved to see that he looked presentable.

Automatically, she followed Giselle through the studio to greet the doctor. He seemed genuinely delighted to be present and looked ten years younger than he had when she last saw him, at his daughter's memorial service. He shook hands with Dale and dropped a kiss on Giselle's cheek, remarking on the bargain he had hanging in his living room. He'd paid Giselle a couple of hundred dollars for a painting of his daughter.

"Excellent judgment," Dale said. "You backed a winner."

She excused herself and left them to talk. This was not the time or place for the frank discussion she needed to have with Francesca, but she wanted to signal her intentions. She glanced around the room, but couldn't see her immediately. Thirsty, she found the bar and asked for spring water. As she waited for the bartender to shovel ice and lemon into a glass, the back of her neck prickled and she was aware of Francesca before she saw her.

"Enjoying yourself?" Francesca asked.

"Yes," Dale replied. "You must be pleased with the turnout."

"I am." Francesca's stare was unnerving. "Exactly the tone I hoped for. Giselle needs to be introduced to the right people. She will never be a Zack Mack, with that rebellious male energy. Giselle offers an enchanting contrast for those who prefer subtlety."

"Like yourself?"

"Ah." She brushed her fingertips over the hand at Dale's side. "You're jealous. Come, let's get some fresh air. I think I can escape for five minutes without anarchy in the ranks." She stepped aside for Dale to precede her through the door, then ushered her up the stairs to the roof the same way.

Already, Dale felt at a disadvantage. Subtly, but unmistakably, Francesca had imposed her will, and objections would seem petty. As gracefully as she could, she surrendered the opening play and followed the dim stairway to the roof. The late June temperature was steadily building toward July. Warm air slid across the city, enervating the plants dotted around outdoor tables and chairs. Giselle had started building a container garden. She imagined drinking iced tea among potted palms.

Francesca removed her jacket. Her white shirt glowed in the light of the low-slung moon. Her eyes were black and glistening. If someone had whispered in Dale's ear that she was sharing the rooftop with a beautiful vampire, she would have agreed.

"Let's not play games," Francesca said, as they strolled to the brick wall that encompassed the terraced patio area. "You're Giselle's lover. I respect that."

"And I respect what you're doing for her. She's flourishing with your encouragement."

"Now that we've declared our mutual regard," Francesca said silkily, "is it understood that we are negotiating terms?"

"Terms for what?"

"Your quiet exit." When Dale didn't react, Francesca said,

"Why waste time pretending? You know as well as I do what we're discussing."

Dale said, "I think the discussion is premature. You only met Giselle a couple of months ago."

"More or less when you did."

"There's no comparison," Dale said. "I'm her lover. I care deeply for her."

"I notice you've made no commitment."

"Giselle was just getting over a breakup when I met her," Dale pointed out.

"Yes, she spoke with me about Bobbi. It's in the past for her." Francesca tilted her head back. Amusement warmed her tone. "I'm not the enemy, Dale. I don't *take* women from their partners. No one can do that. Women don't leave happy relationships."

"I'm a detective," Dale said. "And I can tell you, home wreckers can and do take women from good relationships. They know how to exploit weaknesses. Sex, money, ego…"

"You don't know me, Dale. If you did, you would understand that I cherish my self-respect, and I live according to a code of good manners that precludes what you call home wrecking. Which is why I am talking with you before I speak with Giselle about her future."

Bluntly, Dale said, "Giselle's future is something she and I will discuss when we're ready. In the meantime, I suggest you mind your own business and confine your conversations with my lover to professional matters."

"Are you saying you intend to remain with Giselle in the long term?"

"Yes."

"That's not the impression she gave me."

Dale shrugged, but did not reply, signaling an end to the uneasy conversation.

Francesca looked her in the eye. "I still intend to offer Giselle an invitation. It will be entirely her choice whether she accepts."

"An invitation?"

"To accompany me to Europe for a year to study."

"A year?" Dale told herself to stop repeating every second word.

"Study is essential for her development. She has a remarkable natural gift but has received almost no guidance. She will be taught by the world's best. Is that something you would deny her?"

How could she? Dale's heart felt heavy. When Giselle spoke about studying overseas, Dale had pictured a few weeks in Paris and Florence. Maybe a summer school at a well-known arts institute. She certainly hadn't counted Francesca into the equation.

Maintaining the cool exterior she'd learned on the job, Dale said mildly, "I don't own Giselle. She's free to do as she wishes with her life."

"Then we understand each other." Francesca slid her jacket on. "I appreciate your candor, Dale. And don't worry. While you are with Giselle, I will not be intimate with her."

❖

Giselle lit a slow-burning candle on the nightstand, turned off the lamp, and curled into Dale. "I think Mom liked you."

"She was more impressed with Francesca."

"Old money. Mom thinks people like Francesca are royalty."

"So does Francesca," Dale said dryly.

"She's not that bad. I thought she'd be more of a snob, but she's not."

"You like her, don't you?"

"Yes, she's not like anyone I've ever met."

Dale felt queasy. Francesca was already slowly but surely seducing Giselle, but if Dale said anything her lover would feel distrusted. She would also think Dale was jealous and paranoid, which she was.

Blithely, Giselle said, "I'm supposed to be going to dinner at her apartment on Sunday evening to discuss my studies. Can you come?"

Dale hesitated. "I have to be in Tarrytown. We're having Mom assessed at home for expert testimony."

"I'll ask Francesca to change the day."

Giselle sounded so noncommittal Dale decided she was being overly possessive. If Giselle was interested in Francesca at all, she would want to be alone with her, not trying to make it so Dale could join them.

"No," Dale said. "You don't need me there."

"You'd be bored, anyway." Giselle chuckled. "I know it almost killed you to talk about art all evening."

"I was very proud of you tonight," Dale said, wanting Giselle to know that her accomplishments were noticed. "So was your mother."

Giselle snorted. "Mom's relieved. If I get famous, she won't have to be ashamed of me anymore."

"She's not ashamed of you," Dale insisted quietly. "She's envious."

Giselle rolled her eyes. "Trust me. That's not possible."

"Which one of us is the detective?"

"Okay, you win. But why would you think Mom's envious?" Giselle seemed truly mystified.

"You have what she'll never have."

Giselle giggled. "A lesbian lover?"

"No." Dale was getting impatient. She wanted to have a serious conversation with Giselle, not just banter followed by sex.

Admittedly she needed to make love with Giselle again very soon. Her flesh felt heavy with unspent desire, and her drifting thoughts were constantly snagged by memory. She could feel Giselle's nipples brushing her chest, the hug of her thighs as she rocked astride. She ached for Giselle's mouth. Her clit tensed and she squeezed her thighs together, willing her mind to stay on track and complete what she wanted to convey.

"I'm saying you're an innocent."

"That's not what you tell me when I'm bent over the sofa." Giselle moved her hand down the firm plane of Dale's belly. "Just thought I'd mention it."

Dale arrested the progress of her hand. "You think I'm kidding?"

"I think you've come up with a nice way to say I'm naïve."

"No, that's not it. Giselle, I don't get to see the world through your eyes, and neither does your mom. That's why I like your paintings. I can see what you see. It's magic. I think Nashleigh feels it, too."

Giselle was silent, then said solemnly, "I understand."

Dale kissed her on the forehead. "In my job, most of the innocents I encounter are dead."

"Yes." Giselle hadn't considered how soul-destroying it must be to face the ugliest side of humanity every day. How gray and dirty and barren the world must appear through the lens of disenchantment. She was not a Pollyanna, but she was always able to see beauty. She knew the magic Dale was talking about.

She stared at her lover. Dale's tears in the Tarrytown house had revealed a vulnerability that cut Giselle to the quick. She wanted to know that hidden Dale, the one who could still feel hurt and betrayal. She wanted a window into every dimension. Smiling, she tucked in closer to Dale, oddly pleased that they weren't making love. Sometimes she felt that they had sex instead of talking. Their physical dialogue was so intense, it left little room for anything else.

Giselle recognized that Dale took refuge in sex. That nothing could follow her to that place. She could take herself out of the gray world she occupied and give herself over to sensation and pleasure and release. If only for a short while, she could surrender control. Like most responsible people, she needed time out. Giselle loved to give her those moments. She loved taking care of her, sensually. Massaging her, soothing her, bathing her.

Deeply contented, she moved down Dale's body and listened to the steady rush of her heart. She placed her hand on Dale's breast. How could she explain that Dale had brought beauty and happiness to her, too? She used to feel lost and stuck and ashamed of her own weakness. She seemed to have no control over her life. Everything had changed now. She would never go back to the lesser self she'd inhabited.

She thought about Emma, the friend who had found Ms. Right, and blossomed. One day, at lunch with her and Sandy, Emma had talked about love. About having a partner who wanted her to be all that she could be. Trust between them did not have to be spelled out. Each would find it unthinkable to hurt the other. Emma said, through love, she found out who she really was.

Lying very still, with her heart beating faster than Dale's, Giselle understood that her life had been remade. She was no longer a shadow of herself. Being with Dale changed everything. Marveling, she elbowed herself up so she was a little above Dale and gazing down into her languid gray eyes.

Without a single doubt, she said, "I love you."

And waited.

CHAPTER FOURTEEN

Dale didn't know what shocked her more. Love, sweetly declared. Or the absolute certainty that it was returned in kind. Her heart made its answer known before her mind could frame a denial.

She lifted a hand to caress the downy warmth of Giselle's cheek. Nothing emerged from her parted lips for several seconds before she willed the words to surface. "I love you, Giselle."

"Say it again."

Dale complied very softly. "I love you."

"I didn't mean to ambush you," Giselle said. "I know you're tired, but I wanted to tell you as soon as I knew for sure."

"The timing is fine," Dale said. Francesca could take a hike.

Giselle wriggled up into a sitting position. The single candle burning on the night table burnished her red hair with gold. "I was thinking about how I used to feel…about everything. I was so afraid to kiss you the first time."

"You've made up for that."

Giselle's fingertips idled over Dale's breasts, absently teasing. "What you're really saying is that I've worn you out with my demands."

"Don't stop now." Dale drew her down. Dark copper tendrils slithered through her fingers as she gently steered Giselle's head south. The flesh at her core still felt knotted from the neglect of the past several days. She needed to be soothed into orgasm or something was going to burst. At the same time, she was completely exhausted.

Dale laughed, mostly at herself.

"What's so funny?" Giselle paused to look up.

"I am. Did you set out to make me your sex slave?"

Giselle dragged her tongue over Dale's nipples, one after the other, then softly blew. Her hand drifted down to Dale's center. "Let's see." She placed a fingertip against the taut ridge of Dale's clit and inched it back and forth. Playfully, she declared, "Call yourself frigid? I don't think so."

"I need to sleep," Dale said.

"And you shall. But I want you to come in my mouth first."

Dale's stomach hollowed in Pavlovian response. "Really?"

She watched Giselle's eyelashes sweep down, masking a flash of hunger she knew well. Lips parted, eyes heavy with longing, Giselle slid one leg over Dale's thigh and lowered herself until Dale felt the slippery heat of her center. This was, she thought, how things were meant to be. Love was supposed to include passion, an irrational drive to act on desire, even in the face of complete exhaustion. She should know.

Giselle moved her hips and squeezed her thighs together. Her breasts bounced a little as she rocked. The hand between Dale's thighs dipped lower, gathering fluid. Giselle lifted the freshly coated fingers to her mouth and sucked.

Dale groaned. "Yes, that's what I want."

"I can tell."

Giselle shifted position, moving down the bed until she was on her belly between Dale's thighs. She placed one hand just below Dale's belly to make a resting place for her chin. Innocently, her other hand exploring, she said, "I know you want to fuck me, but you'll have to wait."

She spread Dale a little and took her deep inside. Dale closed her eyes. Already, her muscles were tensing and fluttering. She could come at any moment, but Giselle wasn't going to let that happen. She sucked and tugged, curling her tongue beneath Dale's clit, letting pressure build, then backing off.

Dale's breathing deepened. Her hand dropped to Giselle's head, urging more. She was so tired she didn't have the stamina to hold back the orgasm rushing up on her. "Oh, yeah," she gasped. "Suck me. Don't stop."

Straining, her heart pounding, she felt herself getting tighter and harder. She closed her eyes and lost herself in Giselle's mouth. She pumped into Giselle's mouth, seduced by the tightness and heat. She was coming. An unstoppable stampede of sensation drove her hips up sharply and made her clamp down on Giselle's head. She thrust hard, and a chain reaction overtook her, drawing every muscle into exquisite stress before release.

Dale couldn't speak. Her mouth shook. She let go of Giselle's head and let herself sag completely.

"You kill me," she managed as her labored breathing slowed.

Giselle raised her head and smiled. "No, I love you."

"Come here," Dale said shakily.

She extended her arm and Giselle crawled up the bed to lie at Dale's side. She settled in close, her head on Dale's shoulder, her arm across Dale's chest. "I love that I can do that for you. I love making you come."

"If I had an ounce of energy, we wouldn't be having this conversation. You'd be begging me for more and telling me how I make you feel."

"No one ever made me feel like you do," Giselle said. "When I'm with you, when we make love, I feel beautiful."

"You are beautiful." Dale felt something deep and emotional pass through her. She was disconcerted when her eyes flooded with tears. "I'm so in love with you."

The words shook her. So did the knowledge.

❖

Rich people did not just live in different houses, Giselle thought; they lived on different planets. Francesca's duplex was not far from 927 Fifth Avenue, the building made famous when a pair of red-tailed hawks, Pale Male and Lola, were evicted from their nest overlooking Central Park. Residents offended by twig debris, bird droppings, and pigeon carcasses were surprised when their shabby conduct created an international incident, not to mention a new low by which wealthy cretins could be held in contempt. The nest was eventually replaced with a high-tech version, but the diligent hawks had not successfully hatched a fledgling since.

Giselle's taxi driver pointed out the notorious landmark as they drove by, and passed comments on the heartless villains within. Giselle was glad not to be stopping the car there. Francesca's building was not as ostentatious as the hawk-haters' domain, but the private elevator vestibule was an Art Deco masterpiece that belonged in a movie, and the apartment itself could have been an art museum. Francesca, Giselle had learned, was not just a bank vice-president because she was smart and had a good career; her family owned the bank.

Giselle did not know where to look when the bland-faced British butler led her into a library several times larger than her own apartment. The dark burgundy-toned walls housed works of art that embraced various traditions. She would have been perfectly happy to spend the entire evening viewing them, but Francesca had other plans.

As usual, she was immaculately groomed, but she had chosen a more casual look for dinner at home, wearing a loose-fitting crimson blouse and beautifully cut black pants. It was redundant to notice how they flattered her. Francesca would not make a fashion mistake.

"Your home is beautiful," Giselle said. If her mother could see this, she'd die.

"Thank you." Francesca kissed her on each cheek. Her fragrance was a rich, heady oriental Giselle could not identify.

She must have sensed Giselle's discomfort, because she said warmly, "It's okay. I get overwhelmed walking into this room, and I live here."

Giselle could not imagine an overwhelmed Francesca. She was just being kind. "Did you collect everything yourself?"

The paintings were not the only spectacular collectable. The library was crowded with bronze figurines, porcelain and pottery antiquities, fine furnishings, and clocks. Books were not a central feature.

"I'm afraid I refuse to claim personal responsibility for the looting of Europe in the postwar period," Francesca said. "I've tried to verify the provenance of every piece in this apartment, but my grandfather didn't share my scruples. This was his apartment. My parents live in Rhode Island." She opened a fridge disguised as an oval inlaid-wood cabinet. "Martini?"

"Perfect. Thank you." Giselle sat down in an enormous club chair in front of a fireplace. A rarefied blend of cigars, leather, lemon, and wax tinged the air.

Francesca already had the martinis chilling. Or the butler had mixed them. How did that work? Giselle tried to imagine a knock at the bedroom door each morning and a man coming in with a silver tray on which reposed a copy of *The New York Times*, freshly ironed.

She felt awkward and tongue-tied in this environment and knew she was behaving differently. Francesca always came to Harlem to see her, and Giselle never felt self-conscious when they met in the studio or at a café. She wondered how it must be to grow up in surroundings like these and venture into grimy real-world poverty. Did Francesca feel displaced and anxious? If so, she hid her trepidations well.

Giselle said, "I suppose some of the people who live in this part of town never venture anywhere else."

"That's entirely possible." Amusement glimmered in Francesca's dark stare. "People of little curiosity feel safer when they avoid increasing their knowledge."

Giselle sipped her cocktail and imagined how Dale must be feeling, having an expert asking Mrs. Porter questions she probably couldn't answer. Giselle pictured herself in similar circumstances, if Nashleigh suddenly lost interest in gigolos and no longer knew who she was. The idea was terrifying, Giselle thought in amazement. And dreadfully sad. She gulped a little too much martini and coughed.

Francesca pretended not to notice, but a glass of mineral water appeared at Giselle's elbow seconds later, and she realized the butler must have been standing somewhere in the room. She hadn't noticed.

Wanting to move beyond polite pleasantries to the kind of conversation she usually enjoyed with Francesca, she said, "I had an idea for a series of paintings. Maybe it's a bad idea..." She drank some water. "I don't know if you've ever seen Elizabeth Heyert's photographs—"

"Yes. They're quite wonderful." Francesca moved forward a little in the chair opposite.

"I asked Mr. Owens if I could paint one of his...clientele. Deceased, I mean. Do you think it's macabre?"

"No, I think it's a sellout exhibition." Francesca's fingers floated in an unconscious dance across the leather arm of her seat, and Giselle allowed herself to enjoy the myriad changes in expression that reflected her inner life.

She calibrated each tiny shift, attempting to decode its meaning. Francesca thought she revealed nothing. How wrong she was. "Sit for me?" Giselle asked before she could censor herself.

Francesca regarded her with inscrutable calm. "Yes, but not yet." She inspected her own drink, a martini more clouded than Giselle's, and sipped a modest amount before setting the glass aside. "After Europe, I think."

The idea of studying with some amazing teachers made Giselle flush with apprehension. She would probably be the dunce, the hungry-eyed American with simplistic perception.

She wanted the opportunity but she also dreaded it. What about language? Everyone would probably speak French.

"You're planning to be in Italy soon, I gather."

"Yes." Giselle wondered how much personal information Nashleigh had divulged. Probably too much. "I'll be in Tuscany."

"Your mother invited me to the wedding—"

"She did?" Giselle knew she sounded gauche. Nashleigh hadn't invited Dale. Giselle intended to, but she planned to get her mother's approval first. What would Dale think when she found out that Francesca was already on the guest list? She knew what Nashleigh would say--Francesca was Giselle's patron. Naturally the invitation was appropriate.

"So my thought was, I'll arrange for us to leave well ahead of the wedding date so we can spend time in Florence. After the wedding, we'll travel to Brittany. I think a semester at the Pont-Aven School will serve you very well. We can take a house in the village. It's charming, and the school is an excellent introduction to European study."

Giselle wasn't sure how to ask the question foremost on her mind without sounding rude and ungrateful. Was Francesca seriously planning to accompany her? Dale was going to *love* that idea. "This will take a great deal of your time," she said weakly. "I mean, what about your job?"

Francesca seemed to find this idea highly amusing. "They'd drop dead if I showed up at the bank. I'd probably be arrested for impersonating Francesca Larson. Now, that's a lesson. A simply abominable portrait of me hangs in one of the meeting rooms. Unrecognizable."

Giselle laughed.

"I don't plan to stay in Europe throughout. However, I'll help you find your feet. It's the least I can do."

"Francesca, I don't expect you to pay for all of this," Giselle said. "I spoke with my mother and she'll cover all my costs."

"As you choose. Whatever makes you comfortable."

Relieved, Giselle said, "Dale asked me to give her an itinerary, so we can plan some time together."

Francesca paused. "Dale seems somewhat ambivalent about your plans. I may be quite wrong, but I had the impression that she sees your time in Europe as a vacation with art thrown in."

"You spoke with her?"

"Of course. I don't want her feeling excluded. It's important that she's on your side and understands your needs as an artist. Different career goals so often cause friction in a relationship."

Giselle detected the same tightness in Francesca's voice she'd heard on other occasions, usually when they spoke about relationship woes. Always Giselle's. Francesca hadn't shared her own. Probing, Giselle asked, "Has that happened to you?"

"Not exactly, but I have some regrets. Who doesn't, at my age, if one has led a life at all?"

Francesca seemed smaller suddenly, not a queen but a doll, dwarfed by the huge chair and this room full of objects that had traveled through time to assemble here in this moment. Giselle stared out at a single massive montage woven out of intersecting lives and expectations. If she lived here she would feel weighed down. Smothered. No wonder Francesca wanted to go to Europe.

"I understand her reluctance," Francesca continued. "You're newly together. If you were mine, I doubt I would let you out of my sight, either." Her eyes met Giselle's. She smiled carelessly and rose. "We're being summoned. Let's take the long route to the dining room. I have a Picasso to show you."

CHAPTER FIFTEEN

Giselle climbed the stairs, staring down at the chipped edges and strips of peeling black tread. She paused at the first landing as if she'd been running. In a way she had. Running from the big world with its austere buildings and stony-faced people jostling at traffic lights, compressed between bags of shopping, rushing to get to their tiny, over-priced human storage, high above the streets. To save money, she'd walked a few blocks before beating another jittery refuge-seeker to a cab. She'd forgotten how crazy it was down there.

She found her cell phone and dialed, desperate to hear Dale's voice and know that they could spend the night together. For some reason, she felt afraid. Listening to Francesca describe the new realm ahead of her, the thrills of the journey, the delights to be had in places she'd never seen and didn't belong, Giselle wanted to run away back to Harlem and sit at her kitchen counter with a glass of milk and a Pop-Tart.

Until tonight, the past two months had been in a happy dream. She was content to be carried from one strange chance to another. Nothing seemed really odd. In dreams, who asked why? But in hers, everything was suddenly speeding up and she was being swept along, unable to find a firm footing. Why had she agreed to go to Europe? What was wrong with the schools right here? This was New York City. People from all over the world came here to study.

Francesca spoke as if she had a choice to make: Europe, culture, and a wonderful career with a devoted patron, or staying where she was and hoping for the best. Francesca would still be there, but…disappointed. The real choice, the one Giselle knew she had to make, was between the life Francesca was offering and the one she might build with Dale. If she went to Europe with Francesca, her relationship with Dale would be over.

Dale already had a life. She had her own home. A family, plus family drama. Her job was not just any job. Perhaps she would be understanding and patient and wait for Giselle to come back from Europe. Perhaps she would be willing to put their connection on ice, believing they could pick up where they'd left off. They could try, but there was no pause button in life. There was no going back. Choices and changes were followed by consequences.

Giselle's head spun. If she had not gone back to the dumpster all those weeks ago, she would not have met Dale. Vita's new parents would still be a childless couple. Vita would be dead, and her portrait would never have been painted. Big, important choices were Russian roulette. The outcomes were uncertain. Possible futures were nothing more than wishes and guesses and hopes. If she chose Dale and went to school, and became the best artist she could be, who could say what her life would become? Would she have regrets? Perhaps. But if she made other choices, and lost Dale, one thing was certain. She would be sorr-0y.

Dale's low, even tones calmed her, even as a recorded message. Giselle said, "It's eleven and I'm home now. Please come over. I love you."

"Giselle?" Wrong voice.

Dr. Redman accosted her in the stairwell and demanded, "Have you been watching CNN?"

Giselle almost told the truth: No, I've been eating rack of lamb in a twenty-million-dollar Fifth Avenue duplex with a woman who wants something from me, but I don't know what.

He didn't wait for the socially appropriate alternative answer. "Hurry. It's 'round-the-clock coverage."

Giselle dragged her feet up the stairs after him. "Whatever it is, I really don't think I care."

"I tried phoning you," he said.

"I was having dinner with Francesca Larson."

He nodded. "I did her mother's rhinoplasty."

"Wow." Giselle eyed the sofa in disbelief. "New furniture." People who were planning the long good-night did not buy a lounge suite.

"Forty percent off and free delivery," he said, kicking back in a recliner and aiming the remote.

Giselle flopped down in her usual spot on the sofa with a pillow under her head. In the cat bed under the coffee table, Sheba lay sound asleep with her three kittens.

Dr. Redman was set up for an evening of serious news watching. Popcorn, candy, and soda were all over the table, and he had his pajamas on. The lights were out. He said that made the TV look bigger.

Giselle focused on the screen and immediately understood his keyed-up demeanor. "It's us. The neighborhood."

"W. 119th Street," he said. "Hostage drama."

"I thought there were a lot of police cars on the road," Giselle said. "Unbelievable. It's like a movie."

He turned up the sound and a sorry tale emerged. A man was holding his wife and two children hostage. No one was entirely sure why. Marriage problems. That was the general consensus. Anderson Cooper was on the scene, probably dragged away from another chichi charity-auction bidding frenzy where some eager admirer would fork out $20,000 for his company over dinner.

The action was unfolding in one of Harlem's elegant blocks, where condos were now selling for a small fortune. That probably explained some of the attention the story was getting. Everyone expected something like this in Washington Heights, but not on

Millionaire's Row.

"Dale should be here," Giselle said, trying to phone her again.

"She's probably over there by now," Dr. Redman said. "I heard her come down an hour ago."

"Now you tell me," Giselle grumbled. She peered at the television as if she might see more. The screen was a jumble of patrol cars, special-forces trucks, yellow tape, police, TV crews, and onlookers being herded back.

"I'm going down there," Giselle said.

"No point," Dr. Redman told her. "They won't let you through unless you're a resident."

"How do you know?"

"I live here."

Giselle moped. Why hadn't Dale picked up the phone? There couldn't be much to do, standing around outside an apartment building for hours while a hostage negotiator did his thing.

A photograph appeared on the screen and a CNN anchor in the studio intoned about the man holding the hostages. Married. Yale graduate. Works in mutual funds. Recently relocated. Paid almost $2,000,000 for the apartment.

Giselle and Dr. Redman got up and went over to the television.

"It's definitely him," Giselle said.

Dr. Redman was astonished. "Prizzi."

Every hostage drama has its pivotal moment. For the viewing public, this moment was the shootout. A good hostage drama was supposed to deliver a bang, not a whimper. The ideal ending involved shots exchanged and a hostage-taker going down in a hail of bullets, followed by a SWAT team charging into the house, and five minutes later, the hostages being led out alive and well. A bonus was when the family dog, not seriously hurt, was carried out after them, licking the face of a brawny NYPD hero. Something for everyone.

For Dale and most on-scene officers she'd ever talked to, the pivotal moment usually involved a door. It might open just a crack, and he would be there, trying to fathom how he had arrived at the abyss and whether there was a way out. If a door opened early, hostage negotiators got optimistic. Their guy was engaging. Food could be sent in. A weapon might be thrown out. Doors opening a little wider could mean a hostage emerging with hands on head. A door thrown wide open was a different ball game entirely. The man standing between the pillars was dead or alive in an instant. It all came down to where his hands were.

Doors that never opened at all were a bad sign. By the time the SWAT team smashed them down, the pivotal moment had already happened. People were dead.

Dale had a bad feeling about the solid oak door everyone was focused on. This was not a flashy hostage-taking staged by rival gangs, or a bank robbery turned barricade incident, or a burglar trapped in some granny's apartment, or a jealous-boyfriend melodrama. In these familiar scenarios a tearful jerk was usually taken into custody, thrilled that he hadn't been blown away.

No, the W. 119th Street hostage crisis was a family annihilation in the making. Dale, and every other on-scene officer, just hoped they weren't going to be the annihilators. She and the hundred or so officers who had descended on the scene an hour earlier had closed off the street and established police lines to keep the onlookers at a distance. The last thing they needed was some idiot running into the middle of the street, hoping to get on television or spark an incident.

Within the police lines another zone of safety was designated to put some distance between responders and the emotionally disturbed person holding the hostages. Twenty feet was the norm, and because their EDP was armed and volatile, this was designated a "heavy-vest area," meaning SWAT officers had front-row tickets, one of the perks elite units enjoyed.

Vehicles and protective equipment created a shield behind the heavy-vest area, and there the main players gave the orders. The hostage negotiation team and the precinct commander had just arrived to take over from the patrol supervisor. That meant only one thing: a long night

The arrival of the HNT had sent the signal that this was no longer an incident; it was a drama. Within twenty minutes the place was knee-deep in media, and the hostage-taker guaranteed to be front-page news. Dale wondered if that's what he was hoping for. The most dangerous part of any hostage negotiation was the first ten minutes. That's when the panic reaction set in and it dawned on the hostage-taker that he had set in motion events that were no longer in his control. Some offenders chose that moment to assert control by killing their hostages.

So far, no one had heard any gunshots, which meant one pivotal moment had passed. Dale wanted to leave, but that wasn't going to happen. The NYPD liked to demonstrate a show of strength when they were going to appear in the evening news segments. That meant all-hands-on-deck overkill. Dale would be spending the next few hours milling around with every other cop who could better serve the city by getting a good night's sleep.

She strolled past a line of uniformed officers like she had a purpose and slipped under the yellow tape that cordoned off the police lines. Behind the barriers, members of the public were avidly speculating. From what Dale could hear, discussion centered on two key considerations: could the SWAT team smash into the home fast enough, using the overwhelming force at their fingertips, to rescue the children and shoot the crazy guy? And, this being the 28th precinct, would they smash down the wrong door accidentally and shoot a seventy-year-old deaf black woman who didn't lie down on the floor when her home was invaded by twenty men in terrifying body armor?

The crowd was electrified when they spotted the chief hostage negotiator talking to the commander on the fringes of the heavy-vest area. Here, finally, was the man of the moment, the Denzel

Washington of the W. 119th Street crisis. He had arrived slickly dressed and wearing a Kevlar vest that was not standard issue. His had been customized for a more flattering fit. He was well aware of his starring role and made sure to nod to the crowd.

Dale moved through the spectators without any difficulty; they were eager to step aside for anyone with a badge at an event like this, mindful that if they wanted to stay and gawk, they had to behave themselves. She wasn't the only detective stepping out of the action to phone home.

Giselle greeted her with the enthusiasm Dale normally associated with dogs and small children who expected a gift.

Dale said, "I'm caught up in something at the moment." She didn't want Giselle to start worrying.

Too late.

"Are you on W. 119th Street?"

"Yes, but I'm nowhere near the action."

"Is there some action?" Dale heard a television set in the background. "Dr. Redman and I are watching but nothing seems to be happening. I suppose it's delayed coverage."

"No, nothing's happening. The hostage negotiation team just arrived." She asked the question foremost on her mind. "How was your evening?"

"Interesting." Giselle sounded anxious. "We need to talk. I know now is not the best time."

Dale's hands were immediately clammy. Had Francesca managed to offer Giselle an "invitation" she couldn't refuse? How many hours had passed since Dale had declared her love? Twenty?

"We know the guy," Giselle blurted. "You're the police so we can't tell you everything."

"Be real," Dale said. "This is a life-and-death situation."

"He's a patient of Dr. Redman's."

"A mental patient?"

"No, Dr. Redman isn't a shrink."

"What do you know about him?"

"Not much. He came in for medical treatment the night I found Vita." Muffled noises ensued. Giselle was having a second conversation with her hand over the receiver. "It was a hate crime," she said finally. "A dog chewed off his balls. It wasn't an accident."

Dale's mind instantly zeroed in on Pastor Dunaway and Baldric. Dunaway had referred to a previous incident: *There, I just confessed to beating up a transvestite. Go ahead. Place me under arrest.* Was the hostage-taker, a married man with children, the "transvestite" in question? If so, the negotiator would need to be told. Anything that could provide insight was critical.

"His name is Prizzi," Giselle said. "That's what he told us."

"Can you come down here?" Dale asked. "I think the hostage negotiator will want to talk to you."

"How will I get though? They're not letting anyone in."

"Phone me when you arrive. I'll come get you."

❖

The world turns in seconds, Dale thought. Later, it was possible to go back and identify the beginning of the end, the telltale beats that signaled a calamity to come. At the time, they were impossible to recognize.

She could remember them in relationships. A certain change in voice tone. Lights no longer left on out of consideration for her arrival, late from work. No more meals left prepared in the fridge. No morning hello kiss. No more I Love Yous.

Mrs. Harris must have noticed signs. She must have tried to piece together the mystery of her disintegrating marriage. What would any woman think when her husband, who worked in the financial district, started vanishing late at night and returning smelling of perfume? What had she thought when he stopped having sex with her?

David Harris had been sleeping on the couch in the living room ever since he was attacked. He hadn't been to the hospital. He had decided to hide his injuries. Dale found that bewildering. The victim of a dog attack could expect sympathy and understanding, yet Harris had not sought it. He could have invented some circumstances to explain his late-night absence that evening, divested himself of his dress and high heels, gone to the ER, and his wife would have arrived to find him clean and tidy in a hospital bed.

Why hadn't he used his common sense?

Dale watched as he was stretchered out. There was nothing for her to do. The scene swarmed with police emergency personnel from various units. Just another day in the city.

"Thank God he didn't kill the children," Giselle said as they walked slowly back to Dale's car. Her face was pinched with shock.

"Yes. Thank God."

Harris had done the decent thing. He had spoken politely with the hostage negotiator, encouraging the belief that he was about to surrender. He had then given his wife a 9mm and asked her to kill him. When she refused, he put a second gun to the head of their younger child. He told Mrs. Harris to shoot him first, or he would shoot all of them.

After the single shot rang out, the SWAT team stormed the building. They found Mrs. Harris standing over her dead husband. Dale was relieved that they didn't shoot her on sight.

"It's my fault," Giselle said. "I knew he needed help, but I didn't do anything."

"This wasn't about you," Dale said.

"He was so frightened. And desperate. I tried to talk him into going to the hospital, but he was afraid that his wife would find out."

"You're not responsible. He made his choices."

"And he's dead." Tears quivered on Giselle's eyelashes, weighing them down. "I had a choice. I could have sedated him and taken him to the ER."

"You think this would have played out differently?"

"Maybe."

"There's no point beating yourself up over this. You're not psychic. How could you possibly know what was happening in his life?"

"I suppose I'm thinking about Vita," Giselle said. "I could have walked away. I could have heard a noise and done nothing. I feel like that's what I did with Prizzi. I was going to call 911 but I dropped the phone. Then I just didn't do it."

"David Harris needed more than a 911 call," Dale said. "Ultimately he was the person who controlled his own fate."

The irony of the situation struck her. Harris had escaped death when he encountered Dunaway. He probably didn't know that. Or perhaps he did. Dunaway's arrest had briefly blipped on the media radar. The killing was described as a hate crime and the dog was mentioned. Did Harris read the reports and panic, afraid that the police would come knocking on his door wanting an extra witness? Did he think Dunaway would mention his name, if he knew it? He had already gone to extremes to hide his secret self from his wife. Had he gone off the edge and into free fall believing his cover was about to be blown?

"Collective responsibility applies," Giselle said. "Yes…he made choices and he was responsible for them. But he wasn't thinking clearly. When that happens someone else needs to step up. That's why you're going to become your mother's guardian instead of letting your sister take control."

"Two very different situations," Dale said grimly.

"Yes, but each involves doing what's right and honorable. I didn't do the right thing. I had a bad feeling about Prizzi, but I didn't act on it. What if he'd killed his family, not just himself?"

"That didn't happen. For all you know, you could have called 911 and set off a whole different string of events, and maybe those would have led to a worse tragedy. Then we'd be having exactly the same conversation and you'd be regretting that call."

"You think I'm being dramatic?"

"Maybe a little." Dale smiled. "There's a lot of Monday-morning quarterbacking in my job. You can make yourself crazy with what-ifs. In the end, you just have to accept that there's only so much you can control. Some things are written."

"Francesca wants me to come to Europe with her and study and live in a house in France while I go to school," Giselle said in a rush. "I'd be away for a long time."

"What do you think about that?" Dale asked evenly. She didn't want to create pressure one way or the other.

"It's a wonderful opportunity…I think. Actually, I'm not even sure if that's what it is."

Dale unlocked the car and let Giselle in the passenger side. "What does it feel like?"

Giselle was silent for a long while.

Dale prompted, "Let your gut do the talking."

"I feel like she's collecting me."

Dale nodded. "Well, that's what she does."

"Yes, and I signed up in a heartbeat." Giselle chewed on her upper lip. "There's something else."

At her hesitance, Dale said, "I think we both know she wants to sleep with you."

"She hasn't done anything."

"She has good manners."

Forlornly, Giselle asked, "Do you think that's the only reason she took an interest in me? She just wants to get in my pants?"

"Be serious. Does Francesca look like she can't get a date?"

"No." Relief smoothed her features. With a tight, thin little laugh, she said, "It means a lot to me…what she's done for me. I'm worried about saying no to her."

"About Europe?"

"About anything," Giselle whispered. "It feels so good to have someone believe in me. I don't want to lose that feeling."

"I believe in you. Does that count?"

"Big time." Giselle leaned across and kissed her cheek.

"It's not enough, huh?

"You believe in me as a woman…as me. She believes in me as an artist."

Dale started the car. "Europe is your decision. You can count on my support, whatever your choice."

She glanced down as a sudden pressure constrained her upper arm. Giselle had hold of her with both hands. Her eyes were huge with appeal, making her upturned face seem very small. Her bright hair was untidy from the distracted ravages of her hands. Dried tears formed thin salt tracks that caught the light.

"I can't lose you," she said. "And I can't second-guess. It's too risky. Europe isn't going anywhere, but I couldn't bear it if you did."

"I'm not going anywhere. I promise."

"Then neither am I." Giselle smiled like she couldn't stop herself, a huge grin that made Dale love her so intensely, she could not conceive of life without her.

Dale kissed her, long and tenderly. "My place or yours?"

CHAPTER SIXTEEN

Dale pulled out a chair at her mother's dining table and said, "Sit."

Her sister's bland face darkened and contracted. Penelope wasn't used to that tone from anyone, having insulated herself from unpleasantness her entire life. Dale thought it was time she discovered that behaving like a princess did not make her a real one.

Penelope accepted the chair and said snippily, "You have some nerve, summoning me here like I need to answer to you."

"Get over yourself," Dale said. "This is a family. We answer to one another."

"I don't believe we've had the pleasure." Penelope did not extend her hand to Giselle. "I assume you're my sister's latest nymphomaniac lesbian plaything."

"Correct on all counts," Giselle said.

"What's she doing here?" Penelope demanded.

Dale indicated Carl, chunky and tanned in golf chic. He was ensconced in an armchair in the living room, reading the sports pages. Laurel sat opposite him, eating a bowl of ice cream. Ophelia had gone out to buy groceries.

"Your husband is present. And I've brought my partner."

"Our attorney says this meeting is highly inappropriate."

"Well, duh!" Dale chuckled. "He doesn't get paid if he's not here."

"You've got five minutes to explain what this is about, then we're out of here." Penelope compressed her mouth in bristling indignation. "I can't think of a single reason why we need to talk when we'll be in court in another week."

"That's why we're here," Dale said patiently. She could feel Giselle's hand on her knee beneath the table. She covered it with her own. "You see, I don't want to humiliate you in front of all those people. You're my sister. I'm not sure what you're going through—"

"Menopause," Carl supplied loudly.

"But it's time to end this bullshit. I agree with you about Mom. She's nuts."

Penelope gasped. A veil of smug self-satisfaction descended as if she'd never doubted she was going to win this battle. She was the older sister. Dale had always fallen into line. She said, "I'm glad you're seeing reason."

"I've located an appropriate facility for her. Giselle and I visited it yesterday."

Penelope gave an attentive nod, gracious in victory.

"With your agreement, we'll move Mom out there next week."

"Well, I need to know a little more."

"Such as?"

"Just say yes," Carl said, rolling his eyes.

Penelope did not deign to glance at him. "The cost...the services...I assume the amenities are appropriate."

"It's a lovely place," Giselle said. "Very nice staff. The residents really seem to enjoy themselves."

Penelope ignored her as well.

"I have all the paperwork here," Dale said without inflection. "All you need to do is sign on the bottom line. Mom has already signed."

"As if that means anything." Penelope sneered.

Dale took a calming breath. "What are you saying?"

"That she doesn't have the first clue about any paper she

signs. That's why she's incompetent."

Dale produced a chagrined expression. "I guess we could have saved ourselves the trip, taking her out there and making sure she liked it."

Penelope snorted. "Let's be realistic. Mom could be housed anywhere. It's not like she can play bridge or actually *do* any of the things they do in these places. That type of thing is completely wasted on her." She flipped through the brochure. "I think this is more than she needs. Do they have a basic-care level as opposed to the full package?"

"They do, but I've signed her up for the Alzheimer's package," Dale said. "That's why we picked this place. They specialize."

"I can't believe I'm seeing this." Penelope looked up from her reading. "The Reminiscence Club. Safe and stimulating esteem-building centered on the concept of creating pleasant days. Life skills to preserve dignity. This is completely over the top."

"Come on, Penelope. She can afford it. So what if she doesn't do the club thing every day?"

"I found a facility that provides the basics for half this cost," Penelope said.

"What's the difference?" Dale asked. "It's not your money."

Again Carl piped up. Very slowly, emphasizing each syllable, he said, "It's—not—your—money."

"Stay out of it," Penelope snapped.

Fascinated by her brother-in-law's obstructive attitude, Dale asked, "How are things, Carl?"

"Don't ask me. What do I know? I said I'd give her a divorce."

"You can't divorce my daughter." Laurel finally noticed the conversation.

Carl checked that his hair still disguised his receding hairline, rearranging his salt-and-pepper bangs with his thick fingers. "That's what *she* said, too."

Laurel wagged her finger at Penelope. "You're not trained for anything. You need a husband." To Carl, she said, "Dale is the one who got her father's brains."

Penelope informed Giselle, "Our mother has forgotten that I went to college."

"I'm sure in your day women had fewer options."

Dale stifled laughter. Giselle had spoken kindly and without a trace of sarcasm, but Penelope was visibly fuming. To prevent the inevitable put-down, Dale said, "Penelope had family commitments I didn't have. Now, returning to our discussion, are you willing to sign the papers?"

"I think we're being premature," Penelope said. "After next week, Carl and I will be Mom's court-appointed guardians. We'll make the necessary decisions at that time."

Dale rested her hands on the table, the fingers loosely entwined. "There's something I need to say. We're not going to court. Instead, you are going to sign every paper I have here today, and in exchange I will include you in decisions I make on Mom's behalf."

Penelope's chest rose and fell unevenly beneath the white linen tunic she wore over olive and white striped patio pants. "What *are* you talking about?"

"The tape I've made of this conversation," Dale said calmly.

"You taped this? Without my permission?"

"I don't need your permission to tape a discussion that has also transpired in front of three other people."

"The judge will throw it out."

Dale gave an apologetic grimace. "In a civil case, like this one, the stuff you see on TV doesn't apply."

"Carl?" Penelope stood.

He stayed where he was. "You're screwed. Sign the papers. If we leave now I can still play nine holes."

"Let me make this very simple," Dale said. "When the judge listens to this tape, she's going to hear you being cheap and hard-hearted and your husband mentioning a divorce. She will also hear you say that Mom doesn't know what she's signing. That raises questions about why you had her sign a power of attorney in your favor at the bank recently."

Carl greeted this information with a knee-slap. "Don't tell me. Baron Karan's down payment." Wrapping an arm around Laurel, he said, "Hey, thanks, Mom. You just spent thirty grand on an anniversary party for me and Penelope."

"What party?" Laurel asked.

"You and I won't be there but she doesn't give a shit. It's all about the van Labels." He stood up, not a tall man, but one with plenty of color-panache in his wardrobe. "I'm done, folks."

Dale said, "We're almost through."

He grinned, the face of a long-lost kid still blueprinted beneath the toll of stress and rich food. "No, I'm saying I'm *done*." He started to stroll away, but then made a brisk about-face. "Penelope, you weren't worth it. And something else. You've got no class."

They took their time driving through Tarrytown. Penelope had instructed her attorney that she and Dale would appear in court together to request Dale's appointment as guardian. She'd signed all the papers Dale set in front of her without another word. And she'd concluded the pleasantries of the afternoon by telling Dale that her name would be withdrawn from the guest list for Wayne and Elaine's wedding.

Giselle found it hard to believe Dale and her sister could be so unalike in every way. There was a vague hair color resemblance that Penelope's careful tinting had all but eliminated. Dale's dark-cloud eyes were a similar shape to her older sister's but Penelope had done something to her eyelids. She didn't have Dale's languid stare. They both had good smiles, but Dale's moved her face and was seen seldom enough that it always felt real. Penelope smiled more frequently and serenely but her eyes never warmed.

"What will she do?"

"Frankly, my dear, I don't give a damn."

"What about the house?"

"I'm not selling. I've told Ophelia she can live there as long as she wants. But she's not getting any younger. Maybe I'll talk to her son. Dad left money in trust for her, allocated via the settlement. It's enough for her to get a decent condo somewhere." She cast a sideways glance at Giselle. "Thanks for coming out there with me."

"You did great."

"I'm sorry Penelope was so rude."

"You sister has problems. I didn't take it personally. Carl didn't seem so bad."

"He found some balls," Dale remarked. "Better late than never."

Giselle wondered what the point was in the life he and Penelope had shared. She stared out at the houses and well-kept summer lawns. The late sun shimmered off veils of sprinkler mist. She could almost hear the hiss, and smell the grass. People played in their yards. Kids and dogs ran and yelled. She smiled to herself. She wanted to stake a claim on a future that included those ordinary joys, and she wanted to share it with Dale. It was far too soon to think that way, but the desire to nest-build wasn't new to her. She had wanted a family of her own for as long as she could remember. That was why she'd started painting portraits.

Her first were inhabited by imaginary people. A brother and sister she didn't have. A father who rode a horse and looked like Clint Eastwood. Then she'd painted Grandma Caldwell during a series of prison visits. It was time she went again. Nashleigh never missed her monthly trek to Broward, and made sure the wardens knew she appreciated the good care they took of her momma. She'd been trying to win an appeal against the sentence for as long as Giselle could remember. Giselle wished there was something she could do to make that burden easier. She knew

Nashleigh's worst fear was that her mother would die in a prison cell.

"I'm worried about her," Dale reflected as they stopped for a set of lights. "I only *want* not to give a damn."

Giselle wanted to kick Penelope's parasitic butt for putting Dale through such misery. Diplomatically, she said, "She's the only sister you have."

"If she was young, she could find another rich guy and spend his money."

"I'm sorry about the wedding."

"Christ, I'm not."

Dale started to laugh and Giselle couldn't help but laugh with her. They both rocked in their seats with noisy, spluttering hoots.

"I'm going to drive off the road shortly," Dale said, catching her breath.

"On the subject of weddings." Giselle plunged in. "Are you free to come to Tuscany with me for Mom's? It's next month."

"I've always wanted to go to Tuscany." Dale accelerated onto the highway. "Thank you. I'll put in a leave request right away."

Giselle decided to avoid all mention of Francesca. Perhaps she wouldn't come. And if she did, that was okay, too. There was no reason on earth why she should have a guilty conscience about not doing everything Francesca expected of her.

She said, "Dale, about the wedding."

Dale glanced sideways. Her bone-shaking smile made Giselle's mouth go dry. The rest of her had the opposite reaction, her skin getting damp and the permanent moisture intensifying at her center. She said, "I want to dance with you."

"I'm not really into dancing," Dale replied, not new information.

"You haven't had the right partner," Giselle said. "I want to teach you."

Dale uttered a pity-me whine. "Isn't there some other torture you'd prefer? I'm up for just about anything."

"Do this for me. Please."

"Okay. But only for you."

"I love you," Giselle said.

Dale turned her head and in the very brief meeting of their eyes, Giselle saw in Dale's a yearning so naked she felt like a voyeur witnessing it. The expression seemed to rise from far below the surface as if anchored there. The need it conveyed was not material, or sexual, or emotional.

Dale's soul was reaching out to hers, seeking a home.

CHAPTER SEVENTEEN

Giselle stared into the mirror, unable to look away. Imprisoned in the gilt framed glass, a pearl-fleshed nymph enticed her like a twin she'd never seen. Wrapped in a film of ethereal silk, crowned with a wreath of molten hair, she blinked wide audacious eyes. Full red lips bloomed against her pale, sweet face. Her pale breast quivered. Her neck arched, slender and vulnerable, inviting the mouth of another.

Behind her a lithe, brooding creature stood, eyes burning bare and bright. Stronger, broader, she took the invitation. Her teeth sank into the tender curve. Giselle quivered. Blood like honey, flowed through her veins. Her color rose. When she swayed, the arms she craved wrapped around her. The lover lifted her head, eyes heavy-lidded with lust. A slow languid smile altered her face. One hand explored the girlish contours beneath the silk, the other rested at the narrow intersection of Giselle's thighs.

"You look like you stepped out of a storybook," Dale murmured. "I'm afraid to touch you. I feel like that beast in the magic garden."

Giselle smiled and tilted her head back. "You saw it, too?"

"Yes."

"Like a painting, or a dream yet to sleep."

"Setting aside the fact I'm incredibly aroused, and you're about to be a bridesmaid. While the wedding is happening, I'll be thinking about getting inside you, and you'll be thinking—"

"Ditto." Giselle turned so they were facing each other. "Perhaps we can steal away."

"I'm going to hold you to that."

"It may not be as easy as you think." Giselle recalled Nashleigh's raptor-eyed appraisal of Dale when they arrived from the airport. "Mom has suspicions."

"Um…" Dale cocked her head quizzically.

"She thinks we do more than kiss and hold hands."

"A reasonable theory."

"She hasn't, in the past."

"Parents don't want to see their children as sexual beings."

"I don't know about that." Giselle slid reluctantly from Dale's arms and checked the time. They would have to go down for the ceremony soon. "She's trying to set me up with Fabio's brother."

"Lorenzo?" Dale sounded highly amused.

"What's so funny?"

"Other than how gay he is? Did you happen to notice the male model he arrived with?"

"My mother is a piece of work."

"I like your mother," Dale said. "I think it's time you cut her some slack."

Giselle stifled the reply that first came to mind. She respected Dale. Maybe she could give her some credit, and hear what she had to say. Really trying to understand, she asked, "Why are you on my case about her?"

"Because you have a chance to change things and enjoy each other more." Sadness made her voice throaty. "You still have your mother. I would give anything to have another chance with mine."

❖

The wedding was outdoors in the castle grounds, complete with timeless views of the undulating Tuscan hills. Giselle followed her mother down a central aisle vaulted with ilex and myrtle. Torrents of sunlight seeped like raw butterscotch between the twisted branches, splashing the silvery green lawn. A belt of cypress trees skirted the castle, leading down to row upon row of grapevines. These filed across the valley toward the village, a few steep streets of sun-baked stucco houses, roofs forming a patchwork of gray and salmon tiles.

The sublime landscape had most of the wedding guests enthralled, but a little apart, at the end of a row of seats, a lone figure hung back in the misty shadow of a cypress tree. Giselle knew the elegant frame instantly. Her skin prickled. She could feel the weight of Francesca's stony stare. They hadn't spoken except in the most routine context since Giselle broke the news that she would not be studying in Europe this year. She had told Francesca the truth, that she had fallen in love and could not face being apart from Dale for weeks at a time.

Francesca seemed accepting and she had remained in touch, if distant. Giselle had no problem with that. Francesca's absence had helped her stand on her own two feet. She returned her attention to the other guests, catching Sandy's eye. Her best friend looked like the movie star in this crowd of robustly built matrons. Next to her, also photogenic, was would-be priest Romeo who proclaimed his faith with a wooden crucifix so large airport security would probably confiscate it.

"Slow down," Nashleigh whispered. "Give the photographer a chance."

An enfeebled man weighed down with camera gear, shuffled in front of them. He shot several shaky pictures, then gave Nashleigh a wink and a nod.

"That's Fabio's great uncle Giorgio. He's ninety and still virile."

"That warms my heart."

"You're standing on my train."

As Giselle bent to detach a frill of lace from her shoe, Nashleigh said, "That friend of yours, she's a dyke. The real thing. Just a word of warning."

"Who, Sandy?"

They started the dignified bridal march again. Between toothy smiles, Nashleigh muttered, "No, the detective."

"Mom, as you know, Dale Porter is my lover. And definitely the real thing."

"You don't have to sound so pleased with yourself, missy."

"Can we just walk?"

At the far end of the aisle, Fabio and Lorenzo waited with suitable impatience, occasionally blowing kisses and passing comments to guests in the front rows. Fabio's family comprised large women in black dresses, skinny little old men whose pants were slightly short and held up with suspenders, young hunks, pregnant women in their twenties, nubile teenage girls who had marriage prices on their heads, and countless children. Giselle had the impression they'd probably farmed the same plots of land since the fall of the Roman Empire.

A few of Nashleigh's friends and senior employees, a handful of media, and several important business contacts made up the American contingent. Last night, they'd all headed down to the village to dine and dance. Most were hung over and wearing dark glasses for the ceremony. Giselle scanned their ranks for Dale and they smiled at each other like high school sweethearts.

Nashleigh griped, "Oh, please."

"I'm in love with her," Giselle said.

Nashleigh stopped the slow march in mid-step. Giselle virtually fell into her.

"You're *in love* with her!"

The guests busied themselves translating. Most were not English-speakers. Dale started laughing. So did Lorenzo.

"Every wedding, you just have to embarrass me in front of strangers," Giselle flared, "Well, I've had it." She tore off the rose wreath, a policy-exception she'd made to keep her mother happy. "I'm putting on my jeans."

"No." Nashleigh rushed after her, grabbing her arm. "Please

don't go. I don't care who you love. Just so long as you're happy."
She kissed Giselle on the cheek. Softly, she said, "You've been so
miserable in your relationships, that's all. I thought you should
do something different."

Giselle felt her tension drain away. "I *am* doing something
different, Mom. Have you noticed?"

"Yes," Nashleigh conceded quietly. "And I can see that
you're happy."

"Thank you." Giselle picked up the wreath.

"One more thing." Nashleigh ignored a small warning look.
"You look really beautiful."

Giselle couldn't help but smile at her. Then she and Nashleigh
were hugging, and she said, "I love you, Mom."

Nashleigh sniffed. "I love you, too, pudding."

The shadows grew long. The platters of food came and went
in a constant procession. The waiters were show-offs. Children
marauded around the long tables, yelping and playing. The band,
a small orchestra, played an assortment of Italian songs everyone
knew and sang: opera melodies and Frank Sinatra classics.

Some of the guests had already retired to their rooms to sleep
off the meal. Others were embarking on chess games. Teenage
girls in white party dresses waltzed carefully, holding each other
at arms length so they could watch their steps.

Nashleigh and Francesca were bonding over the delights of
Florence.

"I love the architecture," Nashleigh enthused. "The religious
influence is so…much."

"Yes, completely pervasive," Francesca completed smoothly.
"One must acclimate to angels."

As she conversed, her eyes followed Giselle, glistening
onyx-dark. After a few more words about fountains and marble,
she touched Giselle's hand. "Could we speak briefly?"

By consensus they rose and walked in the fading light. The air smelled of honey and wine. Already Giselle was intensely aware of her companion. They weren't touching, yet the intimacy in Francesca's gaze unsettled her.

"I fear you may have misinterpreted me."

"In what way?" Giselle asked.

"I'm concerned that you've read a personal motivation into my support of your work."

"Am I wrong?"

"Not entirely," Francesca conceded. "My passion for art is quite visceral. It's intense and subjective, like any love. I've found, over the years, that very few of my liaisons understand this. So I've become wary, and sought the companionship of women who are not artists. I've found this…diminishing. Disheartening."

"I can understand that," Giselle replied.

"When we met, I was thrilled. You're gifted, hard working… beautiful. I allowed some of my pleasure to show."

"I've been confused," Giselle admitted. "Things were moving too fast."

"Of course." Francesca nodded. "What will it take to have your continued trust?"

"Let's plan the deceased exhibition," Giselle said. "And I'd like some advice on schools and courses. Let's just get back to…business."

"It's a deal," Francesca said.

They shook hands and Francesca kissed her on each cheek. Without a sign of hesitation, Francesca thanked her and walked away. Relieved, Giselle looked past her to Sandy, who was engrossed in conversation with a television producer from Nashleigh's show. Giselle had met the woman on another occasion. She was smart and real. Sandy gave her a nod and Giselle spoke with the orchestra leader. Several minutes later, they segued into the slow walking rhythm of the Argentine tango.

Dale, deep in conversation with Sandy, obviously wanted to flee, but she stayed where she was. "Are you sure?"

Giselle rested a hand on Dale's shoulder. "Half of them are asleep. You've got nothing to worry about."

The tango was not a complicated dance. The steps were basic combinations. The art lay in the intricacy of the holds and the explicitly sexual dialogue between the two dancers. At different stages, each partner assumed passive or active roles.

Giselle had taught Dale to dance more closely than most Americans were taught. She counted to four and they began to walk the beat, marking the staccato pulse by placing their feet in short stabbing thrusts. The movement was essential to the tension of the dance.

As they fell into flow, gliding and pausing, the closely united pulsation began to play with Giselle's senses and she moved sensually against Dale, murmuring, "You know what I want." She stretched her steps, rolling her butt more firmly against Dale's crotch.

"Yes." Dale held her unbearably close. "Let me take you from behind."

Their bodies slid, angled and deep. Lost in the dance, they turned and slowed. Stopped. Stared at each other. Rocked together, their pelvises aligned.

"My dress is sticking. You've made me so wet I can't dance." Giselle sighed. Her breathing was too fast. She could feel her movements tightening up.

Dale's chest rose and fell hard against her own. Her eyes glittered. She said, "I want to make love. I can't wait anymore. Let's get out of here."

They concluded their dance in a passionate embrace and returned purposefully to the table, amidst applause and stunned faces.

Fabio regarded Dale with an odd mixture of challenge and respect. He told Giselle, "Now you dance with your whole body."

She smiled. "Dale is a good teacher."

CHAPTER EIGHTEEN

Giselle watched, spellbound, as the huge Tuscan moon drowned in a brick red sky.

"Can I tear your dress off?" Dale paced restlessly behind her, tossing her own garments aside.

"People will know what we're up to."

"Yes." Dale's hands were on her shoulders. Her voice was in Giselle's ear. "Are you open and ready? I can't wait."

Giselle left the iron balcony and closed the heavy crimson drapes. She unzipped her dress and stepped out of it as she walked. She was wearing no bra and a pair of silk panties that were more for decoration than practicality.

Dale moved with her, bearing down on her with predatory intent. "You've been teasing me." She pushed Giselle onto the bed and tore the panties aside. "What were you and Francesca talking about?"

"It was innocent." Giselle loved the possessive gaze and the tension in Dale's mouth. Her bottom jaw conveyed so much self-control, Giselle wanted to watch it snap. She said, "It's hard not to think about her naked. She's beautiful."

Dale's eyes blazed with wrath and urgent, helpless desire. Laughing softly, Giselle turned onto her knees and crawled up the bed, as if to get away. Dale's hands caught hold of her hips and jerked her back. Giselle was pulled up, so she was still on her knees but not on all fours. Dale's arms encircled her. Giselle slid her body languorously up and down Dale's, feeling Dale's hard nipples rolling on her back.

Dale's mouth was on her nape. She kissed, softly bit. She groaned. Giselle was pushed off balance, onto her stomach. Her legs were pulled roughly apart. She could smell Dale. She wanted to feel Dale sinking into her mouth. She wanted her face covered, Dale's orgasm running down her throat and smearing her breasts.

She reached behind her. Dale caught her hand, kissed it and returned it, saying, "No. If you touch me, I'll come."

Then she was inside, stretching her, plunging deep. Her breath warmed Giselle's cheek. As she fucked her, she said, "You're mine and I don't share."

Giselle whimpered as sensation consumed her and she was filled until her muscles could no longer clamp down. With one hand, she reached around to the hot, open gateway of her flesh and felt Dale's wrist, completely encircled. Her blood rushed, her breathing faltered. Her mind floated. She let herself go completely, writhing, pulsing, bearing down.

Moaning Dale's name, she squeezed her own breasts, drowned in her own sweat, found in herself a starving, mindless being whose sole focus was her lover's hand.

"I love you," she sobbed. "Only you."

And Dale drove harder, making the final walls crash and her will fall with them.

As she came, she heard Dale repeating, "I love you, Giselle. I love you so much."

Then there was bliss. Complete and entirely theirs.

About the Author

New Zealand born, Jennifer Fulton resides out West with her partner, Fel, and a menagerie of animals. Her vice of choice is writing, however she is also devoted to her wonderful daughter, Sophie, and her hobbies—fly fishing, cinema, and fine cooking.

Jennifer started writing stories almost as soon as she could read them, and never stopped. Under pen names Grace Lennox, Jennifer Fulton, and Rose Beecham, she has published sixteen novels and a handful of short stories. She received a 2006 Alice B. award for her body of work as a multiple GCLS "Goldie" Award recipient, and Lambda Literary Award finalist.

When she is not writing or reading, she loves to explore the mountains and prairies near her home, a landscape eternally and wonderfully foreign to her.

Grace can be contacted at: jennifer@jenniferfulton.com

Books Available From Bold Strokes Books

Vulture's Kiss by Justine Saracen. Archeologist Valerie Foret, heir to a terrifying task, returns in a powerful desert adventure set in Egypt and Jerusalem. (978-1-933110-87-5)

Rising Storm by JLee Meyer. The sequel to *First Instinct* takes our heroines on a dangerous journey instead of the honeymoon they'd planned. (978-1-933110-86-8)

Not Single Enough by Grace Lennox. A funny, sexy modern romance about two lonely women who bond over the unexpected and fall in love along the way. (978-1-933110-85-1)

Such a Pretty Face by Gabrielle Goldsby. A sexy, sometimes humorous, sometimes biting contemporary romance that gently exposes the damage to heart and soul when we fail to look beneath the surface for what truly matters. (978-1-933110-84-4)

Second Season by Ali Vali. A romance set in New Orleans amidst betrayal, Hurricane Katrina, and the new beginnings hardship and heartbreak sometimes make possible. (978-1-933110-83-7)

Hearts Aflame by Ronica Black. A poignant, erotic romance between a hard-driving businesswoman and a solitary vet. Packed with adventure and set in the harsh beauty of the Arizona countryside. (978-1-933110-82-0)

Red Light by JD Glass. Tori forges her path as an EMT in the New York City 911 system while discovering what matters most to herself and the woman she loves. (978-1-933110-81-3)

Honor Under Siege by Radclyffe. Secret Service agent Cameron Roberts struggles to protect her lover while searching for a traitor who just may be another woman with a claim on her heart. (978-1-933110-80-6)

Dark Valentine by Jennifer Fulton. Danger and desire fuel a high stakes cat-and-mouse game when an attorney and an endangered witness team up to thwart a killer. (978-1-933110-79-0)

Sequestered Hearts by Erin Dutton. A popular artist suddenly goes into seclusion; a reluctant reporter wants to know why; and a heart locked away yearns to be set free. (978-1-933110-78-3)

Erotic Interludes 5: Road Games eds. Radclyffe and Stacia Seaman. Adventure, "sport," and sex on the road—hot stories of travel adventures and games of seduction. (978-1-933110-77-6)

The Spanish Pearl by Catherine Friend. On a trip to Spain, Kate Vincent is accidentally transported back in time...an epic saga spiced with humor, lust, and danger. (978-1-933110-76-9)

Lady Knight by L-J Baker. Loyalty and honour clash with love and ambition in a medieval world of magic when female knight Riannon meets Lady Eleanor. (978-1-933110-75-2)

Dark Dreamer by Jennifer Fulton. Best-selling horror author, Rowe Devlin falls under the spell of psychic Phoebe Temple. A Dark Vista romance. (978-1-933110-74-5)

Come and Get Me by Julie Cannon. Elliott Foster isn't used to pursuing women, but alluring attorney Lauren Collier makes her change her mind. (978-1-933110-73-8)

Blind Curves by Diane and Jacob Anderson-Minshall. Private eye Yoshi Yakamota comes to the aid of her ex-lover Velvet Erickson in the first Blind Eye mystery. (978-1-933110-72-1)

Dynasty of Rogues by Jane Fletcher. It's hate at first sight for Ranger Riki Sadiq and her new patrol corporal, Tanya Coppelli—except for their undeniable attraction. (978-1-933110-71-4)

Running With the Wind by Nell Stark. Sailing instructor Corrie Marsten has signed off on love until she meets Quinn Davies—one woman she can't ignore. (978-1-933110-70-7)

More than Paradise by Jennifer Fulton. Two women battle danger, risk all, and find in one another an unexpected ally and an unforgettable love. (978-1-933110-69-1)

Flight Risk by Kim Baldwin. For Blayne Keller, being in the wrong place at the wrong time just might turn out to be the best thing that ever happened to her. (978-1-933110-68-4)

Rebel's Quest, Supreme Constellations Book Two by Gun Brooke. On a world torn by war, two women discover a love that defies all boundaries. (978-1-933110-67-7)

Punk and Zen by JD Glass. Angst, sex, love, rock. Trace, Candace, Francesca...Samantha. Losing control—and finding the truth within. BSB Victory Editions. (1-933110-66-X)

Stellium in Scorpio by Andrews & Austin. The passionate reuniting of two powerful women on the glitzy Las Vegas Strip where everything is an illusion and love is a gamble. (1-933110-65-1)

When Dreams Tremble by Radclyffe. Two women whose lives turned out far differently than they'd once imagined discover that sometimes the shape of the future can only be found in the past. (1-933110-64-3)

The Devil Unleashed by Ali Vali. As the heat of violence rises, so does the passion. A Casey Family crime saga. (1-933110-61-9)

Burning Dreams by Susan Smith. The chronicle of the challenges faced by a young drag king and an older woman who share a love "outside the bounds." (1-933110-62-7)

Fresh Tracks by Georgia Beers. Seven women, seven days. A lot can happen when old friends, lovers, and a new girl in town get together in the mountains. (1-933110-63-5)

The Empress and the Acolyte by Jane Fletcher. Jemeryl and Tevi fight to protect the very fabric of their world: time. Lyremouth Chronicles Book Three. (1-933110-60-0)

First Instinct by JLee Meyer. When high-stakes security fraud leads to murder, one woman flees for her life while another risks her heart to protect her. (1-933110-59-7)

Erotic Interludes 4: *Extreme Passions* ed. by Radclyffe and Stacia Seaman. Thirty of today's hottest erotica writers set the pages aflame with love, lust, and steamy liaisons. (1-933110-58-9)

Storms of Change by Radclyffe. In the continuing saga of the Provincetown Tales, duty and love are at odds as Reese and Tory face their greatest challenge. (1-933110-57-0)

Unexpected Ties by Gina L. Dartt. With death before dessert, Kate Shannon and Nikki Harris are swept up in another tale of danger and romance. (1-933110-56-2)

Sleep of Reason by Rose Beecham. While Detective Jude Devine searches for a lost boy, her rocky relationship with Dr. Mercy Westmoreland gets a lot harder. (1-933110-53-8)

Passion's Bright Fury by Radclyffe. Passion strikes without warning when a trauma surgeon and a filmmaker become reluctant allies. (1-933110-54-6)

Broken Wings by L-J Baker. When Rye Woods meets beautiful dryad Flora Withe, her libido, as hidden as her wings, reawakens along with her heart. (1-933110-55-4)

Combust the Sun by Andrews & Austin. A Richfield and Rivers mystery set in L.A. Murder among the stars. (1-933110-52-X)

Of Drag Kings and the Wheel of Fate by Susan Smith. A blind date in a drag club leads to an unlikely romance. (1-933110-51-1)

Tristaine Rises by Cate Culpepper. Brenna, Jesstin, and the Amazons of Tristaine face their greatest challenge for survival. (1-933110-50-3)

Too Close to Touch by Georgia Beers. Kylie O'Brien believes in true love and is willing to wait for it, even though Gretchen, her new boss, is off-limits. (1-933110-47-3)

The 100th Generation by Justine Saracen. Ancient curses, modern-day villains, and an intriguing woman lead archeologist Valerie Foret on the adventure of her life. (1-933110-48-1)

Battle for Tristaine by Cate Culpepper. While Brenna struggles to find her place in the clan, Tristaine is threatened with destruction. Second in the Tristaine series. (1-933110-49-X)

The Traitor and the Chalice by Jane Fletcher. Tevi and Jemeryl risk all in the race to uncover a traitor. The Lyremouth Chronicles Book Two. (1-933110-43-0)

Promising Hearts by Radclyffe. Dr. Vance Phelps arrives in New Hope, Montana, with no hope of happiness—until she meets Mae. (1-933110-44-9)

Carly's Sound by Ali Vali. Poppy Valente and Julia Johnson form a bond of friendship that becomes something far more. A poignant romance about love and renewal. (1-933110-45-7)

Unexpected Sparks by Gina L. Dartt. Kate Shannon's attraction to much younger Nikki Harris is complication enough without a fatal fire that Kate can't ignore. (1-933110-46-5)

Whitewater Rendezvous by Kim Baldwin. Two women on a wilderness kayak adventure discover that true love may be nothing at all like they imagined. (1-933110-38-4)

Erotic Interludes 3: *Lessons in Love* ed. by Radclyffe and Stacia Seaman. Sign on for a class in love…the best lesbian erotica writers take us to "school." (1-9331100-39-2)

Punk Like Me by JD Glass. Twenty-one-year-old Nina has a way with the girls, and she doesn't always play by the rules. (1-933110-40-6)

Coffee Sonata by Gun Brooke. Four women whose lives unexpectedly intersect in a small town by the sea share one thing in common—they all have secrets. (1-933110-41-4)

The Clinic: Tristaine Book One by Cate Culpepper. Brenna, a prison medic, finds herself drawn to Jesstin, a warrior reputed to be descended from ancient Amazons. (1-933110-42-2)

Forever Found by JLee Meyer. Can time, tragedy, and shattered trust destroy a love that seemed destined? Chance reunites childhood friends separated by tragedy. (1-933110-37-6)

Sword of the Guardian by Merry Shannon. Princess Shasta's bold new bodyguard has a secret that could change both of their lives. *He* is actually a *she*. (1-933110-36-8)

Wild Abandon by Ronica Black. Dr. Chandler Brogan and Officer Sarah Monroe are drawn together by their common obsessions—sex, speed, and danger. (1-933110-35-X)

Turn Back Time by Radclyffe. Pearce Rifkin and Wynter Thompson have nothing in common but a shared passion for surgery—and unexpected attraction. (1-933110-34-1)

Chance by Grace Lennox. A sexy, funny, touching story of two women who, in finding themselves, also find one another. (1-933110-31-7)

The Exile and the Sorcerer by Jane Fletcher. First in the Lyremouth Chronicles. Tevi and a shy young sorcerer face monsters, magic, and the challenge of loving. (1-933110-32-5)

A Matter of Trust by Radclyffe. When what should be just business turns into much more, two women struggle to trust the unexpected. (1-933110-33-3)

Sweet Creek by Lee Lynch. A celebration of the enduring nature of love, friendship, and community in the heart-warming lesbian community of Waterfall Falls. (1-933110-29-5)

The Devil Inside by Ali Vali. The head of a New Orleans crime organization falls for a woman who turns her world upside down. (1-933110-30-9)

Grave Silence by Rose Beecham. Detective Jude Devine's investigation of ritual murders is complicated by her torrid affair with pathologist Dr. Mercy Westmoreland. (1-933110-25-2)

Honor Reclaimed by Radclyffe. Secret Service Agent Cameron Roberts and Blair Powell close ranks to find the would-be assassins who nearly claimed Blair's life. (1-933110-18-X)

Honor Bound by Radclyffe. Secret Service Agent Cameron Roberts and Blair Powell face political intrigue, a clandestine threat to Blair's safety, and the seemingly irreconcilable differences that force them ever farther apart. (1-933110-20-1)

Innocent Hearts by Radclyffe. In a wild and unforgiving land, two women learn about love, passion, and the wonders of the heart. (1-933110-21-X)

The Temple at Landfall by Jane Fletcher. An imprinter, one of Celaeno's most revered servants of the Goddess, is also a prisoner to the faith—until a Ranger frees her by claiming her heart. The Celaeno series. (1-933110-27-9)

Protector of the Realm, Supreme Constellations Book One by Gun Brooke. A space adventure filled with suspense and a daring intergalactic romance. (1-933110-26-0)

Force of Nature by Kim Baldwin. From tornados to forest fires, the forces of nature conspire to bring Gable McCoy and Erin Richards close to danger, and closer to each other. (1-933110-23-6)

In Too Deep by Ronica Black. Undercover homicide cop Erin McKenzie tracks a femme fatale who just might be a real killer…with love and danger hot on her heels. (1-933110-17-1)

Erotic Interludes 2: *Stolen Moments* ed. by Radclyffe and Stacia Seaman. Love on the run, in the office, in the shadows…Fast, furious, and almost too hot to handle. (1-933110-16-3)

Course of Action by Gun Brooke. Actress Carolyn Black desperately wants the starring role in an upcoming film produced by Annelie Peterson. Just how far will she go for the dream part of a lifetime? (1-933110-22-8)

Rangers at Roadsend by Jane Fletcher. Sergeant Chip Coppelli has learned to spot trouble coming, and that is exactly what she sees in her new recruit, Katryn Nagata. The Celaeno series. (1-933110-28-7)

Justice Served by Radclyffe. Lieutenant Rebecca Frye and her lover, Dr. Catherine Rawlings, embark on a deadly game of hide-and-seek with an underworld kingpin who traffics in human souls. (1-933110-15-5)

Distant Shores, Silent Thunder by Radclyffe. Dr. Tory King—along with the women who love her—is forced to examine the boundaries of love, friendship, and the ties that transcend time. (1-933110-08-2)

Hunter's Pursuit by Kim Baldwin. A raging blizzard, a mountain hideaway, and a killer-for-hire set a scene for disaster—or desire—when Katarzyna Demetrious rescues a beautiful stranger. (1-933110-09-0)

The Walls of Westernfort by Jane Fletcher. All Temple Guard Natasha Ionadis wants is to serve the Goddess—until she falls in love with one of the rebels she is sworn to destroy. The Celaeno series. (1-933110-24-4)

Erotic Interludes: *Change Of Pace* by Radclyffe. Twenty-five hot-wired encounters guaranteed to spark more than just your imagination. Erotica as you've always dreamed of it. (1-933110-07-4)

Honor Guards by Radclyffe. In a wild flight for their lives, the president's daughter and those who are sworn to protect her wage a desperate struggle for survival. (1-933110-01-5)

Fated Love by Radclyffe. Amidst the chaos and drama of a busy emergency room, two women must contend not only with the fragile nature of life, but also with the irresistible forces of fate. (1-933110-05-8)

Justice in the Shadows by Radclyffe. In a shadow world of secrets and lies, Detective Sergeant Rebecca Frye and her lover, Dr. Catherine Rawlings, join forces in the elusive search for justice. (1-933110-03-1)

shadowland by Radclyffe. In a world on the far edge of desire, two women are drawn together by power, passion, and dark pleasures. An erotic romance. (1-933110-11-2)

Love's Masquerade by Radclyffe. Plunged into the indistinguishable realms of fiction, fantasy, and hidden desires, Auden Frost is forced to question all she believes about the nature of love. (1-933110-14-7)

Love & Honor by Radclyffe. The president's daughter and her lover are faced with difficult choices as they battle a tangled web of Washington intrigue for...love and honor. (1-933110-10-4)

Beyond the Breakwater by Radclyffe. One Provincetown summer, three women learn the true meaning of love, friendship, and family. (1-933110-06-6)

Tomorrow's Promise by Radclyffe. One timeless summer, two very different women discover the power of passion to heal and the promise of hope that only love can bestow. (1-933110-12-0)

Love's Tender Warriors by Radclyffe. Two women who have accepted loneliness as a way of life learn that love is worth fighting for and a battle they cannot afford to lose. (1-933110-02-3)

Love's Melody Lost by Radclyffe. A secretive artist with a haunted past and a young woman escaping a life that has proved to be a lie find their destinies entwined. (1-933110-00-7)

Safe Harbor by Radclyffe. A mysterious newcomer, a reclusive doctor, and a troubled gay teenager learn about love, friendship, and trust during one tumultuous summer in Provincetown. (1-933110-13-9)

Above All, Honor by Radclyffe. Secret Service Agent Cameron Roberts fights her desire for the one woman she can't have—Blair Powell, the daughter of the president of the United States. (1-933110-04-X)